It's All in the Game

by

Lynne Fox

AN M-Y BOOKS PAPERBACK

A CIP catalogue record for this title is
available from the British Library

ISBN (Print): 978-1-912875-42-9
ISBN (epub): 978-1-912875-43-6

For John Fisher

ACKNOWLEDGEMENT

Thanks to M-Y Books Ltd for their invaluable advice and support throughout the publishing process.

Once again sincere thanks must go to John Fisher for his encouragement and constructive criticism; a very patient man.

Lynne Fox

Annalee Theakston; there's something strangely comforting in using my own name again after so long, it's like regaining my true self, battered and bruised but definitely still me. Those months in St Joseph's Psychiatric Hospital under the care of Dr Metcalfe had given me time to think; to acknowledge my mistakes and plan anew.

I'd had counselling before, long before the accident that had brought me to St Joseph's. Then it had been just a bit of fun; my adversary, for that was how I saw Barnaby, was a rank amateur but our sessions did allow me the opportunity to practise deception, to infer one truth whilst hiding another and to sharpen my memory; it's far too easy to slip up at your next meeting when your adversary is the only one taking notes.

Dr Metcalfe, on the other hand, was a different prospect and a far greater challenge. An eminent psychiatrist with, I discovered, a renowned academic career, he'd concentrated most of his professional life in studying and treating psychopaths, trying to determine if their 'affliction' was more nature or nurture. As if anyone really cares!

Sitting in the window seat of my new apartment I turn toward my beautifully crafted marionette. She has the most compelling eyes, wide blemish-free white ovals, the irises green as ivy leaves with pupils the deep liquid black of its berries. Her lashes, dark brown, are as soft as the ears of a King Charles spaniel and long, so that when she closes her lids they lay against her high cheek bones with the delicacy of an artist's sable brush. I've named her Liliad after the two young women who have so featured in my life; Lily and Addie.

Brushing the marionette's hair back from her forehead I note again the scar and feel the familiar stab of guilt. If only I'd left her at home that fateful evening. I let the hair fall back, covering the blemish and she is once again beautiful, the work of an exceptional craftsman.

As I stare into Liliad's face I know there's no going back, that life can only be lived in a forward gear. The day to day banalities will continue but beneath the reassuring pattern of their normality hides the insidious murmur of compelling desire.

'You know, Liliad nowadays there's a huge profession built up around finding reasons behind people's heinous crimes, as though the human race simply can't accept its inherent evil. Strange, don't you think when the evidence to the contrary is so compelling?'

Liliad's head turns slightly to look out of the window at the crenelated roof top of St Joseph's, one street away and rising like a harbinger of doom over the houses opposite.

'You don't have to worry,' I say, 'we won't go back there, I promise.'

St Joseph's Psychiatric Hospital stands imposingly on the crest of a hill, looking down on the town of Endover like a medieval fortification only instead of keeping marauders out it incarcerates the region's 'undesirables' under the auspices of the 'caring profession'.

My sojourn under its roof was occasioned by a car accident, entirely my own fault for which I paid dearly; broken ribs, broken collar bone but more worryingly, severe head trauma. Put into a medically induced coma for several weeks I was, when considered physically stable, transferred from the General Hospital to St Joseph's for assessment; not just due to the accident but due to my actions and behaviour prior to it, which gave the police and the psychiatric profession reason for concern.

Dr Metcalfe seemed to think he had a need to rid me of my delusions and paranoia but I was well aware that I was neither deluded nor paranoid. I'd known exactly what I was doing but I also knew if I was ever to be discharged I had to play their game. That was OK though; I'm good at playing games.

Seeking revenge on DCI Munroe had become a game, albeit a deadly one. When I was younger I'd dreamt up various ways of killing him, fantasising as to time and place but later I realised that wouldn't be much of a game; it would all be over too soon. I'm not into physical torture although I understand some people find it quite stimulating but no, it isn't for me, at least, not for the present; I lean more toward inflicting emotional pain, the sort that can last for years; that way I get the pleasure of observing my handiwork for longer.

What was Munroe's offence? He ignored me and that I will not countenance.

I'd been nine years old when my brother, Matt's fiancée, Addie Baxter had tragically drowned in what the police initially considered suspicious circumstances. They were quite right, of course although I hadn't actually pushed her in or held her down; I was only nine after all but I had manipulated her into taking a swim in what I knew was a dangerous part of the river. Looking back I'm quite proud of my young self.

Of course nobody was aware of my rôle in Addie's demise, the police attention focussed entirely on my brother. I couldn't have that; the whole point of getting rid of

Addie was to have Matt to myself again so I tried to speak up for him.

Munroe was only a Detective Sergeant, at the beginning of his career, when he'd entered our house that day at the start of his investigations into Addie's death. What was it he'd said, as my mother pulled me out of the room at his request, as I'd tried to defend Matt?

'This is not the place for little girls with wild imaginations. They're merely an irritation.'

Well, I'd shown him just how much of an 'irritation' I could be and I wasn't finished with him yet.

Personally, I blame my parents for everything.

I'd learnt at a very early age that I was an unwanted addition to my family. Six years old, sitting on the stairs at home, I'd secretly watched and listened to my parents in the lounge; even today the image is so sharp it threatens to cut into my psyche like the razor blade cuts I hide under my sleeve.

'If you'd had the snip when I asked you to, she would never have happened. You're so bloody selfish!' Dropping heavily onto the sofa, my mother almost spills red wine on the carpet.

Calmly my father replies, 'It wasn't all my fault; it does take two to tango you know.'

'Don't be so damn facetious; if you'd done as I asked we wouldn't be in this position now. I mean, it's ridiculous; Matt's nearly twenty one with a six year old sister who hangs onto him like some sort of limpet.'

'Matt doesn't seem to mind,' my father replies reasonably.

'Well he should! It's not healthy.' My mother takes another gulp of wine. 'And another thing, there's something not normal about that child; I don't like the way she looks at me sometimes.'

'Oh really, Brenda, now you're just being silly.'

'No, I'm not. Sometimes when she looks at me it's like there's no depth to her eyes; they're calculating – like a cat.'

Moving across to the bureau my father pours himself a large scotch. 'Well, we can hardly put her back, can we? I don't think they have a 'satisfied or return' policy at the maternity hospital.'

My mother gives an exasperated sigh, 'No, more's the pity. I just can't help feeling so resentful; Matt's twenty one and will be off our hands soon; he seems to have taken quite a fancy to that Addie girl he's been seeing so we should be looking, in the near future, to holidays and travelling not standing at school gates and dealing with adolescent tantrums. She's completely spoilt everything.'

The words thrummed in my mind like a stuck record; 'spoilt everything', 'spoilt everything' and then, on top of it all was Munroe, pouring salt into my already livid wound. Oh yes, the revenge I seek is very personal.

◆

I'd focussed my efforts on Munroe's only child, his adored daughter, Lily. I'd had to wait years, into adulthood but patience is the one virtue I do possess, in bucket-loads so playing the long game isn't an issue.

It had all gone really well; I'd manoeuvred myself into a friendship with Lily, manipulated her into a relationship with a young man of dubious character, Barry Mason, who'd been one of my students at the college where I taught; persuaded DCI Munroe that Barry posed an immediate and dangerous physical threat to his daughter and engineered a confrontation that I hoped would result in Lily's death. An eye for an eye; the Old Testament God is much more pleasing, but it all unravelled in the final hour leading to the car accident that almost took my own life and necessitated my enforced stay at St Joseph's.

It was towards the end of my stay in the psychiatric hospital, my discharge imminent, that I had an unexpected visit from Mrs Munroe.

Shirley Munroe was a short, dumpy woman, a striking contrast to her tall, thin husband. Her face was remarkably clear of lines for a woman in her mid-fifties, the skin smooth and healthy looking; the well-scrubbed features of a country girl. Her eyes were small, their narrowness accentuated by her full cheeks so that they almost disappeared in the volume of flesh that migrated upwards when she smiled. She put me in mind of a pot-bellied pig.

Sitting in a chair by the window I stared silently at Mrs Munroe who stood just inside the door, one hand nervously plucking at the strap of her handbag as it lay over her shoulder whilst the other hung down by her side, holding a plastic bag containing … what? I couldn't imagine.

Shirley cleared her throat. 'May I sit down?'

I nodded toward the upright dining chair, the only choice in the room other than sitting on my bed.

Shirley sat bolt upright, her knees pressed primly together, placing the plastic bag on her lap and wrapping her arms around it in a protective, almost motherly gesture. 'I expect you're wondering why I'm here.'

Getting no response she struggled on.

'I know you've been friends for a while now with my daughter, Lily and that you were there when Lily was accidentally shot in the police …' Shirley hesitated for a moment before taking a deep breath and continuing. '… accidentally shot in *my husband's* raid on Barry Mason's cottage. Lily just wanted you to know – well, we both do – that she doesn't in any way hold you responsible for what happened to her. Whatever her father might imply, she believes that you were trying to help when you drove towards them but lost control of your car and she's sorry that you've been so badly hurt yourself.'

Like air seeping out of a balloon, Shirley's body slowly lost its erect tautness as if she'd expelled something that had been caught inside her for a long time.

'Thank you for telling me.' I gave a weak smile, encouraging Shirley to continue.

'The thing is, Annalee, I know you, or rather I know of you from years ago.'

I couldn't control a sharp intake of breath which I hoped Shirley hadn't noticed. 'I don't understand.'

'Like you, I used to live in Dorset, near Bridport; it's where I met my husband; he was just starting out in the police force. My husband, Inspector Munroe, was the investigating officer into that young woman, Addie Baxter's death. She was your brother's fiancée, I believe.'

Sensing Shirley's nervousness I forced myself to keep my face free of all expression but, turning my head to gaze out of the window I said quietly, 'So that's why Dr Metcalfe asked me if I thought, if I saw him again, I'd recognise the policeman who kept coming to our home all those years ago; he was the same one involved in all of this.' I gestured to my bruised body.

'And did you?' Shirley ventured.

'No, no I didn't; I was only nine; the whole episode was so awful I think I must have blanked as much of it out as I could.' I lied; it comes so easily.

Shirley shuffled uncomfortably on her seat. 'It must have been dreadful.'

Turning toward her I allowed a solitary tear to trickle down my cheek. 'My brother, Matt killing himself was the worst; he couldn't believe anyone would suspect him of murdering Addie, he loved her so much ...' Raising my voice a fraction I allowed it to break on a sob. '... but that policeman, he just wouldn't let go.'

'Oh my dear, I'm so very, very sorry. I never would have wished ...'

Pointedly I wiped away the tear. 'Why are *you* sorry? It wasn't your fault.'

'If only I could believe that; I should never have told him.'

'Told who? What?'

'Eddie, I mean, my husband, Inspector Munroe.' Shirley began fidgeting at the plastic bag on her lap, hugging it closer to her breast like a comfort blanket. 'Where we lived, it was such a small community; I knew Addie's mother from one of my evening classes; she often chatted about her daughter and she'd told me that Addie was having some doubts about her relationship with your brother; that there was someone else she'd met and that she was concerned how your brother might react if it ever came to anything. When I met her again, after the funeral, she told me that this other person had amounted to nothing; that Addie was certain she wanted to be with your brother and had been so excited and thrilled at their engagement.'

'I still don't understand why you think you have any blame?'

'Because I *told* him, didn't I? I told my husband that there were problems between the two; that I'd heard that Addie might leave your brother for someone else and that it'd likely cause a lot of anger and resentment. He latched onto it as a motive and wouldn't let go; he was so keen to prove himself, advance his career; he wouldn't listen to anyone after that.'

I let the air hang heavy between us as Shirley's voice trailed into silence. Her admission made my intentions towards the Munroe family even more pleasing. Changing the subject I asked, 'What have you got in the bag?'

Shirley started and glanced down at her lap, as though surprised to find she was holding anything. 'Oh yes, of course, it's for you.'

She held the bag at arms-length toward me but as I made no attempt to take it from her, she struggled up from her chair and, with a slight wince at the stiffness in her knees, crossed the room and placed the bag on my lap. 'It was Lily's idea; I hope you're pleased.'

I made no attempt to look inside the bag but looking up into her face gazed expressionless until she felt so uncomfortable she took a few steps back, as though, amusingly, in the presence of royalty, and resumed her seat on the other side of the room.

Finding it difficult to hide the grin that was threatening to spread over my face I was obliged to look down, automatically opening the bag as I did so. 'Oh!' my surprise was genuine and impossible to conceal.

'She was found in your car after the accident, still strapped into the front passenger seat,' Shirley hastened to explain. 'An arm had become dislocated, probably from the impact. When Lily heard about it she asked DC Wilson to get it for her.'

Shirley fidgeted with the pleats of her skirt as I carefully pulled the doll from the bag, holding her up and examining her closely.

'Lily took her to the doll's hospital, you know, the one in that small parade of shops in the old part of town. They were able to mend her arm but couldn't completely get rid of the gash on her forehead.'

I brushed back the doll's fringe and stared at the scar that ran from the doll's left eye, up and across her forehead into the hair line.

'They've made it a lot better than it was, though,' Shirley continued brightly, 'at least now it's just a neat scar, not the ugly, jagged gash it was before.'

I said nothing, merely let the doll's fringe fall back, covering the blemish and turned to place her on the window cill beside me.

'Of course, I suppose I shouldn't call her a doll, should I? I was so surprised when I saw all the strings; she's actually a puppet, isn't she?'

I snapped back, 'She's a marionette; there's a difference.'

'Is there?' Shirley replied uncomfortably, 'I wasn't aware.'

I found it difficult to hide my contempt at Shirley's ignorance. 'Puppet is a generic term, it can be any one of a number of manipulated dolls; a glove puppet, a hand puppet, a rod puppet but a marionette is the only one manipulated by strings. They have a very ancient and respected history.'

'Well I never.' Shirley attempted a weak smile to cover her feelings of inadequacy. Picking up her handbag she stood and started toward the door but hesitated, obviously deliberating whether to say something more. After an awkward pause she ventured, 'Why did you change your name; call yourself Amelia Thompson?'

I wasn't inclined to answer immediately so looked out of the window as though her question had offended me. Shirley, uncomfortable with my silence, continued. 'My husband says it was because you didn't want anyone to know who you really were; that you were deliberately hiding your connection to your family, to Addie Baxter's death and your brother's suicide. He says it was a calculated ploy to get close to Lily without arousing any suspicions.'

I turned sharply to face her. 'Why would I want to do that?'

Shirley squirmed like a maggot on the end of a fish hook. 'He says it was because you planned to harm her all along; that you knew who he was, I mean, you knew he was her father and also the detective involved in your family's case; that it was a sort of vendetta.'

'Or perhaps I was just trying to forget such an horrific past; put it behind me and have a fresh start. Is that *so* unbelievable?'

I stared accusingly at Shirley, my eyes moistened with tears.

'No, of course it isn't. I don't agree with him and neither does Lily; I'm sure your meeting up and becoming friends was just a coincidence. I'm so sorry; I didn't mean to upset you.' Gathering her coat about her Shirley fussed at her handbag. 'I'd better be going now, you need your rest. Can I tell Lily that you're pleased to have the puppet, I mean, the marionette, back? She'll want to know.'

'Of course.' I watched with a mixture of disgust and contempt as Mrs Munroe left; what a pathetic specimen. I turned to Liliad and smiled, 'I'm so glad you're back; we're going to have such fun.'

CHAPTER 3

I'd been surprised and pleased at Mrs Munroe's candour over what she considered to be her part in my family tragedy. A guilty conscience, the need to atone for one's mistakes, leaves a person open to all sorts of potential manipulation.

I'd known that to communicate openly with Lily would be difficult; DCI Munroe was watching us both like a hawk, but here was Mrs Munroe, a willing go-between, only too ready to salve her conscience. I could hardly believe my luck.

Since that enlightening hospital visit Shirley and I had exchanged mobile phone numbers and by means of coded texts, Shirley had facilitated a couple of meetings between myself and Lily. Those meetings had been brief, both of us tentatively feeling our way back to a relationship that events had severely damaged but once we were both out of hospital and I was established in my new apartment, life settled into a degree of normality and contact between us became easier.

It was a couple of months after leaving hospital that I felt ready to start the game again. I placed a finger under Liliad's chin as she sat on my lounge window seat and gently tilted her head back a little, her eyes opening wider.

'I knew you'd agree,' I smiled contentedly, 'we must get back on track.'

Liliad's head dropped slightly, as though nodding in agreement.

'First things first – another meeting with Lily is called for.'

I picked up my mobile and sent a text to Mrs Munroe.

◆

Four days later, I arrived early at Dougie's café so that I could get a table by the window to watch Lily as she approached and so gauge her mood in advance.

As she rounded the corner, I could tell by her slumped shoulders and drooping head that things were far from happy. Entering the café Lily smiled but her greeting was subdued, measured, no longer exhibiting the carefree exuberance of before.

'Lily, hi.' I indicated the chair opposite, 'I'll get the coffees; what would you like?'

'Oh, a cappuccino will be fine; small please.'

Standing at the counter waiting to be served I looked across at Lily. Her body language displayed a dejection that seemed excessive, even given what she'd been through. Returning with the coffees I smiled warmly. 'It's lovely to see you, Lily. How've you been?'

'OK I guess.'

Staring into the swirls of her coffee Lily absent-mindedly mixed froth and chocolate powder into a brown sludge. With obvious effort she looked up. 'How are you finding your new apartment?'

'I love it; it's so quiet there and the woman in the flat below is very nice although I don't see her much; she seems to work quite long hours.'

'That's good.'

Getting the distinct impression that Lily hadn't really paid attention to a word I'd said, I asked, 'Lily is something the matter? You seem so down.'

Lily gave a brief shake of her head. Trying again, I asked, 'So, how're things with Barry?'

Shit, wrong question! Lily's eyes immediately filled with tears as she fumbled in her handbag for a tissue.

'Oh, Lily, I'm sorry. I didn't mean to upset you.'

Sniffling, Lily took a deep breath. 'It's alright; it's not your fault; you didn't know. We've split up.'

That was a blow; I'd worked damned hard at getting Barry Mason and Lily together; I'd hoped he'd stay around as a thorn in DCI Munroe's side for a lot longer than this.

'But why, I thought you were both so suited.'

'I guess it was all too much in the end; Dad suspecting Barry of being violent, of being a potential murderer and all that questioning. It didn't seem to matter to either of them that it was all cleared up; that Barry's innocence over his father's death was proven; the atmosphere between them was awful; neither of them were able to forgive and forget. And Barry, he's so mixed up about everything. He can't forgive me for not telling him my dad was a DCI let alone the one who was making his life such hell but at the same time he feels it's his fault I got shot; if he hadn't asked me to stay at the cottage with him it would never have happened.'

'Oh, Lily, what a mess.' Reaching out across the table I gently touched her hand in sympathy.

Lily sighed. 'It's no good, there's just too much for any of us to get over.'

'I don't know what to say; sorry hardly seems adequate.'

'There's no need, it wasn't your fault; after all, you were badly hurt yourself; it was Barry's dogs bursting out of the shed and attacking Dad and DC Wilson; none of it would have happened but for that.' Lily shuddered slightly at the memory.

'I know,' I agreed, 'that's why I drove my car at them, I tried to stop them; I couldn't think of any other way; the noise and snarling was so frightening.'

'Yes, but it wasn't their fault, they thought they were protecting Barry and me; it was all just a dreadful mistake and they both paid such a high price for their loyalty.'

'What happened?'

'They were put down, they had to be; Barry was heartbroken.'

I couldn't give a damn about the dogs or Barry. I'd caused the police raid on Barry Mason's cottage, implying to DCI Munroe that his daughter was in danger there. The irony was that if the police bullet had been a fraction higher Lily wouldn't be sitting here and my revenge on DCI Munroe would be complete but now I've got to start all over again; it's so frustrating.

I turned to gaze out of the window, deep in thought as a passing car suddenly backfired. Lily's whole body jerked, her cup dropping from her grasp and clattering onto the table. Picking it up I hastily said, 'I'll get us another coffee.' Returning with a laden tray, 'Here, I've bought a couple of cakes too; I think we could both do with a treat.'

Lily gave a wan smile. 'Thanks.'

'So, where's Barry now? Is he still lodging at the cottage?'

'No, I think he's at his foster parents for now but he's intending to go back up north – he's applied for a job at some animal sanctuary near Sheffield.'

'I see and what are you going to do, Lily?'

Lily shrugged. 'I'm not sure; they've kept my job open at the solicitors but I'm not too keen on going back; I don't seem to be able to cope with pressure anymore.'

'Well, there's no great hurry, is there? I expect your parents are quite happy to support you for as long as it takes.'

She paused and then, as if deciding on something said, 'Yeah, they are. I think I'd like to take up watercolour painting more seriously. I've chatted informally with Madeleine McLevitt, you remember, our bohemian art tutor at college.'

For the first time Lily managed a genuine grin.

'Oh God, yes, she was fantastic!'

'Yeah, she was. She seems to think I have real talent and is encouraging me to take a residential course in Scotland. I might just do that if only because I'm so sick of Dad constantly watching me, I feel like I'm under surveillance.' Lily hesitated, deciding whether to continue. 'I know he's only concerned for me but it's so suffocating; I sometimes think he's got his officers keeping an eye out for me and reporting back.'

'Surely not!'

'Oh yes, even before the accident there were occasions when I felt like he was interrogating me after a night out with friends and he always seemed to know more than I was telling him'

I raised my eyebrows, 'It seems like a stay in Scotland might be a good idea.'

'I know,' Lily agreed, 'when I paint it seems to shut out everything else and Scotland is so beautiful, I want to just be away from everything and everyone. That's what I need right now, some space.' Lily took a large bite out of her cake; for the first time since entering the café seeming a little more hopeful.

Gathering my things, I made ready to leave. 'It's been great seeing you again, Lily; remember to keep me posted whatever you decide, or better still, perhaps you'd like to come over on Sunday, I'd love to show you my flat.'

'I'd love to see it but I can't do this Sunday; how about next?'

'That's fine; I'll get some wine in.'

'Perfect.' Lily stood and we briefly hugged.

'Bye.'

'Bye, Annalee I'll keep in touch.'

Walking back to my car I pondered Lily's news. If she does go to Scotland she'll be well out of my reach a lot of the time but does that really matter? I don't need a long drawn-out strategy now; I realised that when I was in St Joseph's. My relationship with Lily is solid, it can withstand an hiatus and this time I intend for there to be no mistakes; I intend to be much more 'hands-on'.

CHAPTER 4

Returning to my apartment I hugged myself with delight, still absolutely thrilled at getting an apartment I so loved but I'd had to use all my cunning and quite a lot of money to acquire it.

Sitting in the hospital canteen, just before my discharge I'd overheard Nurse Debbie discussing with a friend an apartment on Cranmer Road that sounded ideal. As part of my rehabilitation I was now allowed out for a few hours unsupervised which gave me the opportunity to contact the agents to arrange an immediate viewing. I'd fallen in love the second I'd seen it but the agent turned out to be a principled young man from an old-fashioned firm.

'I think it only fair to let you know, Miss Theakston that we have another viewing booked for three o'clock; a second viewing in fact.'

'But I can proceed straight away; my finances are all in place.'

'I do appreciate that but Lloyd & Sons prides itself on a principle of fair play. The other viewing was booked for four o'clock sometime before you contacted us. I'm sure if positions were reversed you would expect us to honour our commitment to you.'

Seething, I almost choked on my reply, 'I understand, of course. How nice to find a firm with integrity in this day and age. You'll let me know the outcome, I trust.'

'Definitely; I have your number and will inform you immediately. Good day, Miss Theakston.'

Well, I wasn't going to let that little prick stand in my way. Waiting until he was out of sight I retraced my steps and pressed the buzzer of the ground floor flat. I'd noticed, as I'd looked out onto the back garden during my viewing that the tenant of the ground floor flat was home, busily replenishing some bird feeders. She looked to be in her mid- thirties and from her clothing; a pencil skirt and crisp white blouse, a professional woman.

The door opened almost instantly.

'Yes? Can I help?' As she spoke she pulled on a tailored jacket, grabbing a briefcase as she did so.

'I'm sorry to trouble you but I was viewing the upstairs apartment earlier. I wondered if you had any contact details for the landlord.'

'Ask the agents, they'll know. I'm sorry, I have to be going; I've a client in twenty minutes.'

Falling in alongside her as she hurried down the path I tried again. 'Yes, I understand but I just have a couple of questions and it would be so much quicker and easier if I could talk to the landlord direct.'

'OK, I'm not sure he'll help but I don't see the harm; you'll have to walk along with me though.' She rummaged in her case and produced a notepad and pen. Quickly scribbling a name and number she continued. 'He uses the agents to find new tenants but actually manages the properties himself. He's local, a builder so, if you've got any issues with the apartment you tell him and he comes round and fixes things. Only lets to women – says we're less trouble than men.' She gave a slight chuckle as she handed over her note. 'Well, this is me,' she said, stopping outside a firm of accountants, 'Good luck.'

'Thank you *so* much, I hope we'll be neighbours soon.'

Clutching the note, I made my way into the local park and dialled the number. 'Please, please pick up.'

On the fifth ring he answered. 'Terry Watson.'

'Hello, Mr Watson. I apologise for troubling you but I've just been to view one of your apartments; the one in Cranmer Road.'

'You need to speak with the agents about that.'

'Yes, yes I understand but, you see, I really do want that apartment; so much that I'm prepared to pay an increase on the rent and immediately put down six months' rent in advance, rather than the usual three. I told your agent this but he didn't seem too interested, stating that he had another viewing, a second, this afternoon and intended to give her first option in the interests of 'fairness'. I must say, it hardly seems that they're working in *your* best interests.'

There was an interminable pause on the other end of the phone.

'I'm sorry but I don't get involved in choosing tenants; as I said, speak with the agents.' He ended the call.

The bastard! In frustration I thumped the bench I was sitting on; now what?

Back at St Joseph's I pondered my options, realising that I had no time to lose; if I was going to secure that apartment I had to prevent Nurse Debbie's second viewing.

She wasn't involved in my treatment so no-one would expect me to really know her but I'd often observed her from my window on her break, walking to the far side of the garden. There was a bench backed by woodland, quite secluded where she could get away from patients and enjoy a quiet cigarette or two. The weather was fine; it was a fair bet that she'd head for there this afternoon.

Being close to leaving I was now considered such a low risk that I was allowed to wander about the grounds, no-one bothered me. An hour before Nurse Debbie's break was due I strolled across the lawns, wandering by the gardener's shed. The padlock on the door was undone, a slip-up by someone but a godsend to me. Ensuring no-one was looking I darted inside, pulling the door behind me. Stacked against the wall was an array of gardening tools. I selected a small spade then, sneaking out, made my way to the small strip of woodland, hid amongst the trees and waited.

Right on cue Nurse Debbie walked across to her favourite bench and settled down for her daily smoke. I crept close, my feet silent on the carpet of long grass.

Precision was paramount. I had no desire to kill Debbie, she was merely an inconvenience. I raised the spade, brought it back and swung it with calculated force onto the side of her head. The ring of the metal as it made contact with her skull was surprisingly melodious. She slumped to one side before slowly sliding from the bench – a perfect example of someone not knowing what had hit them. A delicious tingling ran through my body that was exquisitely pleasurable; it was a thrill I knew I wanted to repeat.

There was a tap behind the gardener's shed; I washed the spade and replaced it then strolled back across the lawns and up to my room. It was three thirty; I'd leave it until four thirty then ring the agents. As I commented to Liliad, 'It's quite possible the person wanting the second viewing might not turn up.'

❖

'It's surprising how discourteous some people can be.' I remarked to the young estate agent when Debbie failed to turn up for her second viewing. Of course it meant I was able to acquire the flat without having to increase the rent or deposit – more fool Mr Watson!

The house was an imposing Victorian end-of-terrace; I'd been surprised to note that the outside was exceptionally well maintained for a let property; the windows looked clean and the paintwork on frames and the front door gleamed in the bright winter sunshine. The front garden was neat if a little devoid of interest and the pathway, red, diamond-shaped tiles was free of the usual weeds growing between them. The front door opened into a lobby, created by placing a door at the foot of the stairs leading to the top floor and another by its side that formed the entrance to the ground floor apartment. The ceilings were high and corniced with attractive moulding around the central light fittings. The accommodation consisted of a double bedroom looking out over the back garden, kitchen-diner also looking out back, bathroom and a narrow box room for storage. To the front was the lounge with a magnificent bay window taking up the whole end wall beneath which was a padded, deep maroon velvet window seat that followed the curve of the window. Nestled into the corner, her back resting against a matching velvet cushion sat my enchanting, delicate marionette, Liliad, that Shirley Munroe had returned to me at the hospital. I extracted the strings that had been surreptitiously hidden behind the cushion. Lifting them up and entwining my fingers around the string mechanism I made her walk along the window seat but when I stopped her gaze was once more disturbingly transfixed on St Joseph's roofline. I couldn't understand why; after all, it was me that had undergone the therapy.

I'd spent so many hours in Dr Metcalfe's consulting room that I could recall with ease the scent of his leather-topped mahogany desk and matching swivel chair; the aroma of freshly ground coffee from the gurgling machine that sat in constant readiness on the corner unit; the cosiness of the background lighting lending intimacy to our time together and Dr Metcalfe himself; a compact man, muscular in an understated way and always immaculately dressed; dark grey suit, bow tie and a jacket lining which flashed deep red silk as he moved; a statement of his self-assurance.

He was always solicitous toward me, more than simple doctor patient courtesy, of that I was convinced. The physical damage caused by my car crash, the ugly bruising and shorn scalp had slowly healed and now my natural beauty shone through. I'd kept my dark hair short, in an elfin, impish style that framed my features and accentuated my high cheek bones. That, coupled with my petite frame meant I always looked younger than my years which leant a vulnerability to my appearance, something men seemed to gravitate towards,

I lowered my head slightly, looking up at Dr Metcalfe at a slight angle, my eyes wide and innocent; an endearing look I'd perfected over the years.

'Another two weeks, Annalee and I believe I'll be able to sign your discharge papers. You've made excellent progress, how do you feel about going back into the world?'

Sipping slowly at the coffee he handed me I considered my response. 'A little nervous but excited too. I think I'll feel better when I'm back in work.'

Dr Metcalfe's smile was reassuring. 'Have you been in touch with the hospital administration? They can help you with the practicalities.'

'Oh yes, they've been very helpful; they've got me a job interview next week.'

Seeming grateful was diplomatic but in truth, I considered the job was an insult to my intelligence and abilities. As I complained to Liliad, 'It's a "meet and greet" receptionist at the Conference Centre; a well-trained chimp could do it! I've got a degree in Art History and teaching qualifications; don't they realise that?'

Slumping down on the sofa I tossed the application form onto the coffee table in disgust. Liliad merely looked at me; eyes wide and challenging. I poured a glass of merlot and took a couple of over-large sips. 'What do they think, that I can't manage anything more demanding?'

Looking at Liliad's impassive face I sighed and continued slightly sulkily, 'Well, I suppose it won't take up so much of my time as teaching at college did, so I'll have more time to play the game, won't I? That's got to be a plus.'

Liliad didn't respond.

CHAPTER 5

As far as I was concerned the job was the best of the very poor selection on offer and initially I was tempted not to apply. I wasn't desperate for the money as my parents had recently signed over to me the monies they'd kept in trust for my deceased brother, Matt. It was a considerable sum our parents had intended to give him as a wedding gift. They'd hung onto it in a separate account so it'd accrued quite a bit of interest over the years. It came with a solicitor's letter coldly informing me that it was a once and for all gift and that they were emigrating with no forwarding address given.

So be it, they were no loss.

However I knew that in order to keep the authorities off my back I had to show willing so I figured I'd go for the interview but deliberately perform badly until, that is, I saw the place.

Westbridge Conference Centre formed part of a luxury hotel complex on the outskirts of Endover. Set in one hundred and sixty five acres of parkland it boasted exquisite views over a large lake where a variety of water fowl lived an idyllic, tranquil existence.

I couldn't believe my luck; never having been there before I'd no idea what to expect; it was beautiful and I immediately changed my mind about the job. Sitting waiting for my turn I looked around the room and assessed the potential of the other candidates, deciding there was only one who posed a possible threat. Immaculately dressed in a light grey skirt suit, patent leather shoes with matching handbag, the young woman exuded an air of confidence and professionalism that, coupled with an easy, ready smile made a winning combination.

Wandering across to a table where various leaflets about the complex and its facilities were displayed I picked up a couple at random and moved back to sit in the vacant chair next to the young woman. Turning the leaflets over, I casually remarked, 'I didn't know the hotel gave clay pigeon shooting tuition; have you ever tried it?'

The woman looked a little surprised but politely responded, 'No, I haven't; I don't think it's really my thing.'

'Probably not mine either. My name's Annalee, by the way.'

'Hi, Josephine.'

Glancing around the room I said, 'I hate this waiting; has anyone gone in yet?'

'Yes, a couple; what time were you given?'

'Two thirty, what about you?'

'Two o'clock so not much longer, hopefully.'

Rummaging in my bag I produced a pack of mints; holding the packet out to Josephine. 'Want one?'

'No, I'm fine thanks; be glad when this is over though. Have you applied for many jobs?'

'This is the first, well, for a while; I had a bit of a car accident so I've been out of commission for a few months, I've now got to get back on track.'

Josephine looked genuinely concerned. 'I'm so sorry; it must be difficult for you.'

'I'm getting there. How about you, have you been out of work for long?'

'I'm actually in work but it's a standard nine to five job whereas this will involve a certain amount of flexibility. I know they hold quite a few evening events as well as the daytime conferences and symposiums; I'd like the variety.'

I feigned surprise. 'So, you don't mind this being only a temporary position?'

'Temporary? I didn't know it was.'

'Oh, I'm sorry, I probably shouldn't have said.'

Josephine's concern was evident. 'No, please tell me.'

Leaning in closer, I whispered, 'Well, I've a friend who works up at the hotel and she told me. Apparently, although this is part of the hotel complex up to now the hotel have franchised out the running of it but they've now decided to take it over; they feel they've enough staff; receptionists, concierges, porters etcetera; they plan to start interviews of their own admin staff shortly and to run it themselves. The current franchise ends in three months.'

Josephine looked horrified. 'But why haven't they made that clear for this job?'

'I expect it's because they want to ensure a certain calibre of applicants, don't want to risk standards dropping in the interim and remember, the probation period will undoubtedly be about three months. At the end they'll just say you didn't come up to scratch and end your employment at next to no cost to them.'

'God, that's awful. I can't afford to give up a secure position for something so tenuous.'

Josephine started to fidget in her seat, obviously trying to make a decision, so I continued. 'It doesn't matter so much to me; I'm not worried about it being short term as it's not something I want to do for long; it's just a stepping stone after my accident to help me back into work but if you're already in a decent job it's a very different prospect, isn't it?'

'Yes, it is a very different prospect and I'm not wasting my time on an interview for something so short term.'

Picking up her bag and coat Josephine stood and turning toward me, 'I wish you luck though.'

'Thanks; I hope things work out for you too.'

Just then the door to the inner office opened and a middle-aged woman called, 'Josephine Turner, please.'

'I think she's just left; I'm not sure why.' I offered.

'And who are you?'

'Annalee Theakston.'

The woman glanced at her list. 'Well, it seems you're next then, Annalee; would you follow me please?'

Monday morning, my first day at the new job, couldn't have been more delightful. A sharp frost covered everything, the needles of the fir trees looking so much like they'd been coated with crystallised sugar I was tempted to pull some off and pop them into my mouth. A thin film of ice covered the edges of the lake but was clear of the frost so that I could see through it, like looking through a thin sheet of glass to the gently swaying fronds of pondweed and milfoil. I even spotted a water boatman rowing speedily along on his back and couldn't help smiling as I watched the coots placing their strangely lobed greenish-grey feet delicately, in pigeon toe fashion, as they treaded carefully toward open water.

Standing for a few moments, breathing the cold, clean air into my lungs I consciously relaxed my body before turning toward the front doors of the Conference Centre.

Inside I was greeted by a smartly dressed woman whom I gauged to be in her late twenties. Her blonde hair was short but expertly cut just above the lobes of her ears, drawing the eye to her sparkling earrings. Tall and slender, she carried herself with an air of easy authority that was professional but far from intimidating.

Holding out her hand she introduced herself, her voice carrying the soft burr of Scots origin. 'Annalee, my name is Robyn Campbell, the Events Organiser; that's Robyn with a 'y' by the way,' she gave a wry grin, 'in my time I've been called Robin Redbreast, Robin Reliant, asked where Winnie is…'

I frowned, puzzled at this last.

'Christopher Robin – Winnie the Pooh.'

'Oh, I get it.'

'Yes, so did I as I grew up; over and over again. There were times I hated my parents,' Robyn chuckled gently, 'but I thought I'd just get it all out of the way to start with.'

'Surely no-one comments on it now?'

'You'd be surprised; the number of bullies in business suits who still haven't left the playground is quite staggering. You'll come across quite a few during the course of your work but just smile sweetly and you'll be fine. Now, I'll show you the essentials; the ladies cloakroom, the canteen and the reception area where you'll be stationed, then we'll grab a coffee and I'll run through what I need you to do today. I'm afraid I'm going to have to throw you in at the deep end a bit as we have a conference scheduled for tomorrow afternoon involving all the top mental health consultants for the three counties so that's about fifty delegates all of whom require name badges, place markers and information packs put together. Do you think you'll be able to manage that?'

'I'll do my best.'

Robyn nodded, 'I can ask no more but don't hesitate to give me a shout if you get stuck on anything; my office is just over there.' She pointed toward a door to her left. 'Now, let's get those coffees and we'll get started.'

By the time five thirty arrived I was exhausted; I don't think I've ever worked so hard so consistently but I felt a tremendous sense of achievement as I observed the pile of name badges and place markers; childish I know, but very satisfying! The majority of the information packs had been photocopied and correlated so I should be able to get that finished tomorrow morning quite easily.

I was just collecting my coat when Robyn walked across. 'Well done, Annalee; I'm impressed; if you continue like this we'll get along fine.' Robyn paused. 'I know this is a big ask so soon into a new job but I've just been let down by one of the girls who was meant to be handing round the wine and nibbles at the end of the conference. Could you help out with that as well, please; it'll mean a bit of overtime?'

'Yes, of course, no problem.'

'Brilliant.' The relief on Robyn's face was clear. 'Otherwise I have to miraculously be in about three places at once! OK, get home now and rest; you deserve it.'

◆

Arriving home on a complete high I slung my bag and coat onto the sofa and pirouetted into the kitchen diner to grab a bottle of Chenin Blanc from the fridge. Balancing the bottle and a glass in my other hand I waltzed back into the lounge and plonked onto the window seat beside Liliad.

'It was great; I've had a super day. My boss is really easy to get along with and the work, although very busy, isn't exactly rocket science but, do you know the best bit of all?' I take another sip of wine, pausing for maximum effect. 'The best bit of all is that I've seen the list of delegates and Dr Metcalfe will be at tomorrow's conference so it'll be easy for me to renew his acquaintance especially as Robyn, that's my new boss, has asked me to stay on into the evening to help hand round the drinks and canapés when the conference has finished.'

Taking hold of Liliad I gently adjusted her sitting position, inadvertently causing her head to turn slightly to gaze once more out the window at St Joseph's. It was uncanny the way her head always seemed to turn in that direction.

I shivered slightly and took another large sip of wine, noticing with surprise that I was already a third of the way down the bottle. 'Whoops! Better slow down and get something to eat; I think I'll buy in a pizza and then have a bath and an early night.'

I leant forward and gently touched my lips to Liliad's cheek.

Although the conference wasn't due to start until three thirty delegates begin arriving from two o'clock onwards with a huge influx around the three o'clock mark so that I was inundated with handing out name badges, providing coffee, giving directions and generally shepherding men in suits who didn't seem to understand the simplest of directions. Robyn came over at one particularly swamped period and gave me a hand and it wasn't until things had eased a little that I realised that Dr Metcalfe's name badge had gone. Damn! Robyn must have dealt with him whilst I was busy with someone else. I'd have to grab an opportunity later when the conference was over.

Six in the evening and I'd morphed from receptionist into wine waitress. Trying to locate Dr Metcalfe amidst a sea of suits wasn't easy, especially as I stand at only five feet three.

Spotting him in the far corner of the room I felt a pleasurable anticipation. He was in animated conversation with an elderly gentleman whose white hair, beard and portly belly made me think of Father Christmas.

Weaving my way through the throng, carefully balancing my tray of drinks, I manoeuvred until I was standing slightly behind Dr Metcalfe's left shoulder. 'Drinks gentlemen?'

Father Christmas reached out eagerly and seized a glass of red wine but Dr Metcalfe merely glanced in my direction, gave an almost imperceptible shake of his head and immediately turned his attention back to his companion, continuing what he was saying.

I remained where I stood for a few seconds, feeling a mixture of embarrassment and anger. Has he not recognised me? I hesitated for a moment longer before asking, 'Perhaps I can get you something else, Dr Metcalfe; would you prefer a coffee or tea?'

I smiled warmly as Dr Metcalfe turned to face me and said in a determined tone, 'No, thank you,' and immediately turned back to his colleague.

Feeling quite stupid I moved away, the tray wobbling precariously as I fought to hold back the anger surging inside.

'Are you OK, Annalee? You look done in.' Robyn took the tray from me. 'Why don't you go home, it's all winding down now anyway, several of the delegates have already left.' Robyn smiled and layed a comforting hand on my arm, 'You've had a bit of a baptism of fire for your first few days at a new job. Get off home, I can manage the rest.'

'Thanks, Robyn; I am a little tired.'

Gathering my things, I could feel my insides still trembling at Dr Metcalfe's slight, shocked that he could ignore me in that way, as if I were nothing, a nobody.

Taking a deep breath I made my way out into the cold night air. Slinging my handbag onto the passenger seat of the car I turned the ignition, putting the heater and fan onto full blast while I waited for the condensation that always freezes onto the inside of the front windscreen to clear a little; an aggravating downside of my aging car.

Now that the adrenalin rush of the past couple of days was over I realised just how tired I was. I settled back a little, relaxing down in my seat and closed my eyes for a few seconds while I waited for the visibility to improve before driving off.

A sharp tap on the side window startled me; my eyes immediately wide open I struggled into a more upright position and turned toward the noise. Dr Metcalfe was leaning down, his face framed in the window.

'Are you OK, Annalee?'

I rolled the window down. 'Yes, I'm fine; just waiting for my screen to clear.' I indicated in front of me, 'It's always a problem during the winter months.'

Dr Metcalfe, his voice full of concern said, 'I just wanted to explain why I didn't acknowledge you in there.'

I said nothing, merely stared at him, waiting.

'If I had, it might give rise to questions from other delegates and even perhaps, from some of your work colleagues who happen to notice. You don't need that, Annalee, not when you're just rebuilding your life; it isn't anyone else's business what's gone on in your past but, in my experience, it's always better to avoid any probing; where possible don't give rise to speculation. I hope you understand.'

I paused as if considering the wisdom of his words. 'Yes, yes of course; thank you, Dr Metcalfe.'

'Anyway, I'm glad things seem to be going so well for you; you seem to have really found your feet. Well done, Annalee.'

His smile warm and reassuring he stood up from his slightly crouched position at my car window. 'Drive carefully now and keep up the good work.' With that, he turned and made his way across the car park to his Mercedes.

I watched him go, fuming at his patronising attitude; waiting until he'd got into his car and driven off before switching on my lights and pulling out.

◆

Back in my apartment, I lay supine on my sofa having just finished dinner washed down with a copious quantity of Chablis. My mood was pensive; Dr Metcalfe's explanation just didn't wash, not one iota. What does he take me for? Does he think my brain is addled? He wasn't trying to protect me it was simply that once I'd left his care I was no longer of any significance or use to him. How could I have possibly once believed otherwise?

I think back to my time in St Joseph's; all those sessions in Dr Metcalfe's consulting room. The subdued lighting, cosy atmosphere, tantalising aroma of freshly brewing coffee, his solicitous, kindly manner; all designed to put me at ease, get me to open up, let him in to my most private thoughts; ostensibly to help me.

I snorted in derision; yeah, right; more likely to gather material for his research; an example to illustrate his latest academic paper. He'd used me; I was nothing more to him than a laboratory rat, something to be prodded and poked, assessed, labelled and disseminated amongst his colleagues.

I look across at Liliad, sitting on the window seat, silently observing me. At least at night, with the curtains drawn, she can no longer keep her gaze fixed on St Joseph's.

'I've been a fool, Liliad; I thought for a while Dr Metcalfe really liked me but I was wrong, wasn't I?'

As I stare, Liliad's eyelids seem to flutter slightly, the pupils of her eyes shining with a dark intensity, reflecting the flickering flame of the imitation log fire.

'I don't like being made a fool of and I *won't* be ignored. He thinks he's so clever, that he set me on the straight and narrow path of the sane. His arrogance is astounding. I think we ought to show Dr Metcalfe just who he's dealing with, don't you?'

Liliad's head drops slightly forward in the semblance of a nod or perhaps it's just the effect of a sudden draught from the badly fitting bay window. I made a mental note to call my landlord to have it repaired.

CHAPTER 7

S unday and Lily is due to arrive any moment. I must play this very carefully. I've been thinking a lot about her and have decided that she needs to go on that art course in Scotland. I need her isolated from family and friends; it will make my task so much easier.

The shrill of the doorbell startled me. Lily stood at the door clutching a bunch of freesias. 'Here, I thought you'd like these; the scent is heavenly.'

I took the flowers and put them to my nose, inhaling their heady scent. 'Thank you, Lily, they're gorgeous and the colours are wonderful.' Turning I beckon Lily to follow me up the stairs and into the kitchen. Rummaging in a cupboard for a vase I plonk the flowers into water. 'I'll sort them properly later; coffee or a glass of wine?'

'Coffee to start with please, maybe the wine a little later.' Lily gives a cheeky grin as I nod my approval. She's changed since I first knew her; all that bothered her then was her dad's opinion of her behaviour and drink was a definite no go area. These subtle changes under my influence are very pleasing.

'This is a nice room.' Cradling the mug of coffee in her hands Lily wanders about the kitchen diner taking everything in. 'There's plenty of room isn't there and the window overlooking the garden is really nice. Do you have use of the garden?'

'Yes, it's a communal space but I don't tend to bother too much. The landlord comes once a month and cuts the grass and generally keeps it tidy but the woman in the ground floor flat, Carol, she uses it more. They're her bird feeders you can see. Come on, I'll show you the rest.'

The inspection over, we sat side by side on the lounge sofa enjoying glasses of wine from the bottle, already two thirds empty, that stood on the coffee table.

'Have you thought any more about that residential art course you were telling me about?'

Lily sighs, 'Yes, lots but Dad's the problem.'

'Can't you get your mum to work on him? Perhaps she could get Madeleine McLevitt to talk to him; assure him of its credentials and pastoral care set up.' I've decided I really need Lily to go for this; I must get her away from her hawk-like father. 'How long's the course?'

'A year; it's based at some retreat type place in the very north of Scotland; I get my own en suite room and designated place in the studio; there are lectures and seminars as well as loads of practical sessions.'

'It sounds ideal; you have to make this happen, Lily.'

'I know, I've got the application form and Mum says she'll give me a cheque for the initial deposit.'

'Then just do it; if you've got your mum's backing you'll be fine.' I paused to allow a note of sadness in my voice. 'I shall miss you though.'

'I shall miss you too,' I didn't think she sounded particularly sincere, 'but I won't be gone that long; I'll be back for the holiday breaks.'

I noted that she made no suggestion that I might visit whilst she was there, the bitch.

At that very moment Liliad suddenly lurched forward off the window seat, crashing onto the floor with a clatter of wooden limbs. We both jumped, startled by the sudden noise.

'Good grief, whatever happened?' I rushed across to Liliad, gently picking her up and examining her closely.

'Is she damaged?' Lily's concern was genuine.

'No, she seems OK; I guess I couldn't have set her far enough back on the seat; she must have slipped.'

Lily glanced at her watch. 'Gosh, is that the time? I'd better be getting back. Thanks for the wine and everything; I've had a lovely afternoon and I think your apartment's super.'

Walking into the kitchen diner to collect her coat and handbag she returned to the lounge, watching as I repositioned the marionette carefully against the cushion. 'You're really fond of her, aren't you?'

'Yes, I suppose I am. I found her when I was spending a weekend in Brighton; she was in one of those little curio shops in The Lanes. She was sitting in the window and I found I just couldn't walk past; it was her eyes; I felt like she was compelling me to go in and buy her. I didn't realise she was a marionette until I got inside; I thought she was just a wooden doll.'

Lily moved a little closer to the marionette, studying her intently. 'She is exquisite, incredibly well made.'

'Yes, she is; the longer I have her the more I appreciate just how unusual she is. Marionettes have been around for ages; they were used to tell stories before there were actors.'

'Really?'

'Yeah, apparently Homer's poems, the Iliad and the Odyssey were first presented using marionettes.'

'Wow, that's incredible, I'd no idea.' Lily leant down toward Liliad, staring intently into her eyes, 'Well, young lady, it seems you have illustrious ancestors.'

Liliad stared back, her expression unresponsive but her eyes glistening like sun on a raven's wings. Lily took a sudden step back as though she'd just received a mild electric shock, her focus still on the marionette, but her expression disquieted. With some effort she gathered her coat around her. 'Thanks again for a lovely time, Annalee.'

'You're welcome, I enjoyed it too. Keep me posted on the course application; I'm sure you'll have no problem especially with your mum on your side and Madeleine McLevitt's recommendation.'

'I do hope not, I'm really looking forward to it now. Bye.'

A brief hug and she was gone, the only evidence of her existence being the freesias in my kitchen diner. I leant on the table and slowly pulled the petals from the stems before breaking and crushing the bunch between my hands. I picked up the waste bin and brushed the torn and bruised flowers off the table into it. If only Lily could be disposed of so easily.

I returned to the lounge, glancing across at Liliad. 'Oh hell, work tomorrow, let's hope this week isn't as busy as my first one; it'll be good if I get some time to myself to consider what we can do about Dr Metcalfe.'

CHAPTER 8

It seemed like forever but eventually the working week was over and I sat with Liliad on Friday evening, pondering matters.

'Liliad, you know Dr Metcalfe has a fiancée, a Melissa something or other; he had her photograph on his desk.' I paused remembering the strikingly pretty young woman in the picture frame. 'I've been thinking, perhaps Dr Metcalfe needs to be taught a lesson.' I gave Liliad a knowing grin, gathering up the strings in my hand and hop, skipping her along the seat.

Setting her on my lap, facing toward me, I continued. 'Yes, I think Melissa could well be the answer.'

Staring hard at Liliad, I could see my own reflection staring back at me from the deep black pools of her eyes. Mesmerised, I watched as my reflection seemed to recede, like Alice falling down the rabbit hole.

I shuddered slightly as I replaced her onto the window seat, carefully tucking the strings behind the cushion. 'Tomorrow's Saturday, I think I need to start laying the groundwork for Dr Metcalfe. Lily can wait until I visit her in Scotland; then I can give her my undivided attention.'

Saturday morning was grey with a fine mist of rain that fell with the gentleness of snowflakes but without their dancing beauty to offset the misery of being wet through. I gazed out of my bedroom window deciding whether to bother with spying on Dr Metcalfe today or putting it off until the weather got better. Eventually I decided on making myself a cooked breakfast and then going out. 'Who knows, the weather might have improved a bit by then.'

By ten thirty the rain had eased although a damp chill hung in the atmosphere; bushes drooped heavy with moisture and next door's cat, picking its way daintily over the back garden lawn, left indented footprints in the sodden ground.

Wearing my green wax jacket, the hood pulled up and a scarf wrapped outside it around my neck, I pulled on gloves and forced myself out the front door. I decided not to take the car; Dr Metcalfe's apartment block was only one street away and, although the car was a far more inviting prospect than standing out in the cold I didn't want any chance of him noticing me.

His apartment, close by St Joseph's Hospital, was on a much busier road than mine but its saving grace was that directly opposite, instead of a row of houses, was a large park consisting of the usual kids climbing apparatus, several football pitches regularly used by junior clubs and a narrow strip of woodland surrounding the entire area.

Entering the park I positioned myself just inside the woods facing out toward the road where I had a clear view of the apartment block's entrance doors and set myself a couple of hours to wait; if nothing happened I'd go home and think again. It being the weekend I was, to some extent, banking on him meeting up with his fiancée; past experience has proved that sometimes opportunities simply turn up; you just have to be in the right place at the right time.

Stamping my feet and flapping my arms to stave off the numbness I could feel creeping into my fingers and toes, I barely moved from my vantage point; a gap between the trees. I'd been there just over an hour when I noticed a small, grey Fiat turn into the car parking area in front of the flats. A young woman in her mid-twenties stepped out, her calf length red woollen coat striking, making a splash of exuberant and defiant colour against the greyness of the day.

Walking up to the entrance doors she pressed one of the buzzers, waited a few seconds her head tilted slightly to one side, then spoke briefly into the receiver before pushing the door open and disappearing inside.

I cast my mind back to my time in Dr Metcalfe's consulting room, trying to picture the woman in the photograph on his desk. It could be the same person but she was too distant; I'll need a closer look to be sure. One positive is that I can see Dr Metcalfe's Mercedes in the car park so he's probably at home, so there's a chance that it's him the woman is calling on.

Knowing I couldn't stand around in the cold much longer I took the decision to walk across the road, note the Fiat's registration number and then walk to St Joseph's and pay a visit to Nurse Betty Fletcher, my main carer during my stay in the hospital. I'd promised to keep in touch with Betty when I'd been discharged but that was as far as it'd got; it was about time I renewed that acquaintance as I might be able to glean some useful information.

Keeping my hood up and my head down, just in case Dr Metcalfe's apartment looked out over the car park, I hurried across the road. The Fiat was parked close to the building in a visitors' bay shielded by cars in the rows in front of it causing me to have to walk right into the car park, threading my way between vehicles, to get a clear view of the number plate.

Just as I got close enough to begin committing the number to memory I heard the main doors open and ducked down beside a Range Rover as Dr Metcalfe and the woman came out and, to my relief, turned away from me toward the Mercedes. Convinced now that I'd had a closer look that the woman was indeed Dr Metcalfe's fiancée, I relaxed a little and began to stand up from my crouched position when Melissa suddenly turned and walked toward her car, calling over her shoulder, 'It's in my car, Andrew; I'll just fetch it.'

Crouching back down as Melissa opened her driver's door, my heart pounding with the fear of being noticed, I heard her rummage on the passenger seat before emerging with a large envelope, locking the door and retracing her steps.

Afraid to move, I stayed hunkered down where I was until I saw the Mercedes drive out of the forecourt.

'What are you doing down there?'

Startled, I shot upright to find a fat man in his sixties dressed in a three quarter suede jacket and driving gloves; he had a definite air of pomposity about him and was looking at me with barely concealed annoyance and suspicion.

'I dropped my keys.' Covertly I put my hand in my pocket and dangled the keys as evidence. 'Found them!'

'Mmm, well this is private property; unless you live here or are visiting, you're trespassing.'

Bridling at his superior attitude I retorted in kind. 'I can assure you, I am not trespassing. I've just been to visit Dr Metcalfe, a friend of mine, who you may have noticed has just left which is why *I* am now leaving.' Tossing my head haughtily skyward, I walked past and out onto the road, muttering just loud enough for him to hear, 'Arrogant bastard!'

Entering the main gates of St Joseph's I felt a fluttering of anxiety in my belly; it was the first time I'd been back since my discharge and memories of my physical injuries and the probing by Dr Metcalfe into my mental state rose to the surface and, for a brief moment sickened me; to have felt that vulnerable is not something I wish to repeat.

Pausing on the path I looked up the steps toward the imposing entrance doors; so tall and solid, built of a dark wood with minimal austere relief work they offered a hypocritical welcome which, like a prison, is a greeting no-one entering ever wanted.

Taking a deep breath and mentally shrugging my shoulders to relax I stepped up to the doors, turning the large metal ring handle. The latch clunked, echoing through the entrance lobby as I pushed against the door, my shoes clacking on the speckled grey floor tiles; the familiar smell of cleaning fluids and antiseptic assailing my nostrils as I walked toward the reception desk.

The young woman looked up from behind her computer screen. 'Hello, can I help you?'

'I wondered if Nurse Betty Fletcher was available; it's just a social call.'

'I'll try for you.' The woman looks at her watch, 'it's almost one o'clock; she's probably on her lunch break so you might be in luck. What name shall I say?'

'Annalee Theakston.'

'I'll try paging her first.' We both waited in silence for a few moments until the receptionist's intercom rang. 'Hi,

Betty, there's an Annalee Theakston in reception would like to see you. OK, will do.' She looked up, 'she says she's in the canteen if you'd like to join her. Do you know the way?'

'Yes I do; thanks.'

Turning I headed down the corridor toward the canteen. A pleasant room, one wall was almost completely glass looking out onto the grounds. This time of year the gardens are somewhat sparse but neatly tended, the dark soil glistening with moisture, looking as rich and nutritious as Christmas pudding.

I spotted Betty Fletcher immediately, looking crisply efficient as always; there was a comforting cuddliness to Betty making her seem like everybody's favourite grand-mother. When I was really poorly I felt I'd like to snuggle into her ample bosom like a child. God knows there'd been no maternal affection in my childhood.

Betty looked up as I entered, a welcoming smile that reached her eyes in genuine pleasure.

'Hello, dearie, how lovely to see you, how've you been?' she stood and gave me a brief hug as I neared the table.

'I'm OK thanks; got my own flat and a nice job at the conference centre.'

'Oh, I'm so pleased; I knew you'd come right in the end; veritable little fighter you are!'

I smiled, I'd not thought of myself like that before but Betty was right, I am a fighter and I'm not finished yet. 'How are things with you, Betty? Are you very busy?'

'I'm afraid we're always busy in this place, dearie.' Betty sighed, a wistful look on her face, 'too many stresses on people these days, especially the youngsters.' She shook her head, sorrow evident then brightened up. 'But you've come out of it OK, haven't you, dearie?'

'Yes, Betty I have, thanks to your care and Dr Metcalfe's. How is he by the way?'

Betty smiled, 'Oh, he's fine, getting married in September to a lovely girl; I've met her on a couple of occasions, very sociable she is; do him the world of good she will; he spends far too much time here to my way of thinking.'

'Oh yes, I remember seeing a photograph on his desk. Is she called Melissa?'

'That's right, Melissa Hartnell.'

'I remember, is she local?'

'Yes, born and bred here from what I understand.'

'Do you think they'll move away when they're married?'

Betty seemed surprised at the question. 'Why ever should you think that? No, Dr Metcalfe is too dedicated to this place and Melissa's a teacher at Walker Street Primary School. No, they'll stay local for sure,'

Just then Betty's pager sounded. 'That's me, no rest for the wicked. It's been lovely to see you again, dearie; will you keep in touch? I'd like that.'

'Of course I will.' I stood too. 'I must also get going, take care, Betty.'

'You too, dearie, you too.'

Stepping outside, the weather had changed again and a sharp north easterly wind was throwing stinging rain into my face as I hurried down the entrance steps. Pulling my hood up and holding it close to my face to protect my cheeks from the onslaught I scurried out onto the pavement and headed for home. Walking along, my head bowed down, I re-visited my conversation with Betty. So, Dr Metcalfe's wedding is in September that will give me enough time and Melissa works at the local primary school; it'll be easy to follow her from there and find out where she lives. Yes, things are coming together rather nicely.

CHAPTER 9

Arriving home I'm so intent on getting up to my flat to get warm and dry, I almost missed the envelope left on the hall table. It only bore my name, no address so it must have been hand delivered; I didn't recognise the writing either but gave a slightly dismissive shrug. I''ll have a look as soon as I've got my wet clothes off and made myself a cup of hot coffee.

I entered the kitchen diner and placed my jacket and scarf on the back of a chair to dry while I made the coffee. Walking through into the lounge I put the fire on full blast to quickly take the chill off the room.

'It's cold out there now,' I said to Liliad, 'you're defi-nitely in the best place, the wind's bitter.' I opened the envelope. 'Oh, it's from Lily; she's got a place on the art course; great! She goes in a couple of weeks.'

Settling on the window seat I picked Liliad up and placed her on my lap. 'Things are coming together nicely.' I gazed into her eyes and was surprised at their intense gleam, like the sheen of highly polished ebony.

By the evening, sitting snug in my dressing gown I turned to Liliad again. 'I popped into St Joseph's to see Nurse Fletcher; the one who mainly looked after me. She tells me that Dr Metcalfe is due to get married in September and that his fiancée works as a teacher at Walker Street Primary so it's going to be a doddle now to find out where she lives.' I paused, reflecting, 'I've decided I'm going to have a bit of fun with our Dr Metcalfe and his fiancée before the final act; let him know what it's like to have your mind messed with.'

I drew my legs up onto the sofa and wrapped my arms around them, hugging myself with delight. 'It's going to be such a great game!'

◆

Towards the end of the following week I wasn't feeling a hundred per cent; the chill I'd picked up standing out so long in the cold and damp at the weekend seemed to have stayed with me so I decided to take a couple of days sick leave. Although not absolutely necessary, coupled with my eagerness to begin work on destroying Dr Metcalfe's relationship, I decided a little white lie to Robyn was justified.

Thursday afternoon at three o'clock I made sure I was sitting in my car outside Walker Street Primary School, waiting. I could see Melissa's little grey Fiat in the staff car park and although I didn't expect her to leave when the kids came out I didn't want to risk missing her by arriving too late.

I parked a little way back so as not to draw notice to myself but found that the conglomeration of parents' cars and the tidal wave of screeching kids hurtling out of the playground completely blocked my view for a few minutes. Craning my head toward the staff car park I was dismayed to see, through a brief break in the crowd, that the Fiat was no longer there. 'Shit!'

Starting the engine I pulled out but was immediately stopped by the school lollipop lady shepherding a group of toddlers and their mothers across the road. 'C'mon, c'mon.' my hands twitched on the steering wheel in exasperation. As the lollipop lady turned back to the school-side pavement I pressed my foot onto the accelerator and shot forward.

A loud THWACK echoed through the car. Slamming on my brakes I gulped down the sickening fear that surged through me as an irate mother thumped on the bonnet.

'What the hell do you think you're doing? You almost killed Albi. Back your bloody car up.'

Too shocked to do anything else, I slowly reversed a few feet as the woman bent down near my front wheel and came back up holding a flattened satchel that was leaking orange liquid out of its split seams.

'I should report you,' the woman shouted holding up the ruined satchel, 'look what you've done to his satchel.' Grabbing a young boy by the hand she stomped across the road, dragging the boy behind her.

I sat where I was for a few seconds, a mixture of relief and disbelief wafting over me. A tap on the side window broke my stunned state; I turned to see the lollipop lady beckoning me to lower the window.

'Try not to be too upset, love; it wasn't all your fault. The little devil threw his bag under your car in temper when his mum refused to take him to the shop to buy sweets. He's a little tyke and she's not much better although you were a bit quick off the mark outside a school.'

I nodded my acceptance of the gentle criticism. 'I know, I'm sorry; got a lot on my mind.'

'I know, easy done. Just drive careful in future.'

'I will; thanks.'

Slowly and with deliberate caution, I pulled away, my heart still thumping as I neared the T-junction.

My plan to follow Melissa now a complete non-starter, I decided to pull in at the local shops and treat myself to a small bottle of brandy for the evening. I could do with something to calm my nerves.

Leaving the express supermarket clutching brandy, milk, a mixed salad and a moussaka I wonder, yet again, why I can never go into a shop and stick to the one item I'd gone in for. Making my way back to the car I unexpectedly spotted Melissa's Fiat parked in the far corner near the hairdressers. Hurrying to put my bought items in the boot, I walked back past the hairdressers' window. Yes, she was there, I could see her near the front of the shop obviously having a cut and blow dry and not much longer to go by the looks of it. Great; perhaps not everything is lost after all.

Retracing my steps I settled into my driver's seat to wait. Thirty minutes later Melissa walked out of the salon to her car. I pulled carefully out behind her, the afternoon's episode still fresh in my mind and followed at a distance as Melissa manoeuvred out into the traffic.

◆

Later that evening, sitting once more on the window seat, I run through things with Liliad. 'She lives in Cadogan Square, not far from the town centre. It's a quite posh looking apartment block; hasn't been built long by the looks of it. I don't yet know which is her apartment; I didn't want to risk drawing attention to myself by wandering around but I'll pop over there tomorrow when she's at school and see what I can find out. They've probably got names by the entrance door buzzers, most small apartment developments do, at least the modern ones.'

I took a sip of brandy and glanced across at Liliad. 'You never really liked Dr Metcalfe, did you? Was it because he picked up your strings and tried to walk you after Mrs Munroe had brought you back to me at the hospital? It was presumptuous of him, I agree and he left you in a tangled heap on the floor, as I recall.' I gave Liliad a sly grin. 'It wasn't a nice thing to do, was it but we'll pull his strings soon enough so you'll get your revenge.'

Liliad's eyes sparkled as I took another sip of brandy.

CHAPTER 10

Next day I drove over to Cadogan Square around ten o'clock, parking in a layby on the far side of the Square so as not to be directly outside the apartment block. Stepping out of the car I paused for a moment, taking a general look at the area. It really was very pleasant here, my impression admittedly being influenced by the sunshine that made a welcome relief from the previous day's rain and wind. It was still cold but clear, sunlight sparkling on raindrops as if the black railings that surrounded the block were encrusted with diamonds.

The Square encompassed an enclosed grassed area with a small fountain in the centre circled by four benches. There were a few neatly tended flower beds, their tilled soil awaiting a spring planting whilst multi-coloured crocuses, thrusting up through the grass, nodded their heads slightly in the gentle breeze.

As I'd driven in I'd noticed that the building on the corner plot at the entrance to the Square had been turned into a rather chic café. I strolled slowly around the central garden making my way back deciding to have a coffee first.

Opening the door to a rather melodious set of chimes I was welcomed by the aroma of freshly ground coffee and a pleasant smile from the woman behind the counter.

'Good morning, may I have a flat white please?'

'Of course, take a seat and I'll bring it over.'

Settling myself at a table by the window I found I had an uninterrupted view of the apartment block's entrance door which was in a direct line with the fountain. Each of the apartments on the first and second floors had a private balcony edged with a waist high wall for protection. If Melissa had one of those I could imagine her sitting out on a warm summer evening with a glass of wine gazing down onto the Square and fountain below. I felt quite nauseous with envy.

I glanced up as the woman placed my coffee on the table and noticed that she also was gazing out of the window at the display. 'It's really pretty, isn't it, with the sun shining through the spray.'

She smiled. 'Yes, it is. I never tire of watching it.'

'It must be lovely for the people in that apartment block, the one's whose windows look out this way.'

'Yes, I've often dreamt of living there myself but they're a bit out of my price range.'

I nodded. 'Mmm, I know what you mean. Do you get many people who live in the Square popping in here?'

'Yes, quite a bit. We're more of a restaurant in the evenings getting quite a bit of custom from people going to the theatre; the Square seems to have a lot of "culture vultures".' She grinned, a very slight touch of sarcasm in her voice.

'Oh, of course,' I exclaimed, 'I'd forgotten that the theatre is so close.'

'Yes, it works well for us. Organic snacks and light lunches during the day and evening meals on most nights. Here,' she walked across to the counter and came back, handing me a menu. 'We've quite a good selection; have a look.'

'Thanks.'

'Of course,' she continued, 'we're also quite happy for people to just pop in for a drink; we're becoming quite a meeting place.'

As if on cue the door chimes rang out as a mother entered, threading her way between the tables with a pushchair.

'Hi, Maggie; coffee and freshly pressed juice for Simon?'

'Please; God, I need to sit down.' The mother sighed as she sank gratefully onto a chair.

The waitress moved back behind the counter and I resumed my appraisal of Melissa Hartnell's home. As I pondered my next move an idea started to form in my mind. Basically so simple yet it could prove very effective and I'd enjoy watching the situation develop; all part of the game.

Finishing my coffee, I thanked the waitress and left.

Turning toward town I'd just recalled that there was a market on Fridays and this one had an excellent flower stall. I didn't want to use a shop florist as they sometimes keep records of purchases and customers but I knew buying from the market would be an anonymous transaction.

It being the very end of February there wasn't a huge amount of choice but the stall keeper managed to construct a delightful bouquet of winter blooms, neatly finished off with a deep red ribbon.

'Do you want to write a card with it, luvvie?'

'No, I'll be handing it personally so no need.' I paid and, barely able to suppress a grin as I thought of the confusion it would cause, I walked briskly back into Cadogan Square.

Reaching the apartments I scanned the buzzer name plate noting that Melissa's apartment was number ten on the second floor. I pressed the tradesman's button but the door didn't respond. Checking my watch I realised with dismay that it was past twelve noon, probably the cut-off time. 'Damn!' As I hovered, uncertain now what to do, I jumped as a man's voice asked, in sonorous tones, 'Can I help?'

Looking in the direction of the sound I noticed steps to my left hand side, leading down to a basement flat. 'Oh, you startled me; I don't know if you can. I need to leave these flowers for Flat Ten but there's no response.'

'I can take them in for you if you'd like.'

'That's very kind but I've been told to leave them outside the apartment if no-one's in; they're in water so they'd be OK. Can you open the main door?'

'Yeah, I don't see why not. Hang on a minute while I get my keys.' He ducked back inside and a few seconds later emerged dangling a set of keys from his fingers.

Stocky, with a round, boyish face he sprinted up the steps, surprisingly agile and grinned, 'Feel like a jailer with this lot', he commented, 'main front door, laundry door, bin store, my front door – all that for a tiny, one-bed apartment! There you go, open.'

I smiled gratefully. 'Thanks so much, I'll just pop up and leave these outside the door.'

'No problem' and he'd gone, leaping back down the steps four at a time.

The entrance lobby to the apartments was well presented; a mahogany table sporting a vase of fresh flowers and a few leaflets of local events and places of interest. To the left of the table, affixed to the wall, was a bank of locked letter boxes for the individual flats.

Entering through the second set of doors the area opened out with the ground floor apartments on either side of a carpeted staircase that rose centrally up to the first and second floors. Number ten turned out to be situated at the front of the building, looking out over the fountain and directly above the entrance lobby. My envy grew; the lucky bitch!

The front door of number ten was recessed a little so that I was able to prop the bouquet safely with no threat of it being knocked by clumsy feet. Suddenly my mobile rang shattering the silence. Hastily I grabbed at it, desperate to shut off the noise; it was Robyn from the Conference Centre. 'Annalee, it's Robyn; I was just wondering how you are and if you'll be in to work on Monday.'

'Oh yes I'm feeling much better, thanks.'

'Good. I didn't mean to push you but we've a busy week coming up and if you weren't going to be in I really do need to organise temporary cover.'

'No, it's fine; I'll be there.'

'Great, have a good weekend.'

Placing the phone back in my handbag I was about to go back down the stairs when I heard the front doors open. Oh no, the last thing I want is to be seen here and even worse, by Melissa. I glanced around the landing but there was nowhere to hide. I stood stock still, dreading the sound of footsteps on the stairs but I was in luck; thankfully it was someone on the ground floor. Once I'd heard their door close I hurried down the stairs and out to my car. It had been unfortunate that the chap in the basement apartment had seen me; I'd hoped not to be noticed at all; any encounter held a potential threat of association when events began to unfold but there was nothing I could do about it now. Hopefully, our meeting was so brief he'd dismiss me from his mind and recall very little about me.

CHAPTER 11

The weeks passed amazingly quickly, mainly due to my job at the Conference Centre being so busy.

In fact I was so busy I'd have missed Valentine's if it hadn't been for my having to take in a huge bouquet on the day for Carol, my downstairs neighbour. I dashed out to the Hotel Chocolat shop and bought a large box of specialty chocolates, had them wrap it in hearts and flowers paper and drove round to Melissa's apartment.

Arriving whilst the tradesman's entry system was still working I raced up the stairs, placed the gift outside her door and hurried back down, pulling up my jacket hood and keeping my head down as I exited just in case the chap in the basement apartment was about. The last thing I needed was for him to recognise me as a frequent visitor.

Dropping onto the window seat next to Liliad on my return I gave her a gentle nudge. 'Phew, that was close;

I almost missed the opportunity to cause trouble. I shall have to call on Melissa soon, find out how her relationship with Dr Metcalfe is going.'

Being so busy I hadn't had time to think about Lily. She'd been in Scotland for almost two months and at the beginning she'd emailed often telling me every detail of her accommodation, the area and the course but recently I'd noticed that her emails were getting shorter and less frequent. I'd sent a couple of texts asking how she was but she'd taken ages to respond and even then, without much information. I'd even suggested that perhaps we could plan dates for me to visit but she'd been particularly evasive. Not happy with the way things seemed to be going I contacted Mrs Munroe on the pretext of wanting to discuss ideas for Lily's birthday that I knew was soon. We arranged to meet in Sainsbury's café.

Mrs Munroe was already seated at a corner table when I arrived, her hands clasped possessively around a large mug of latte and a huge slice of half eaten chocolate gateau in front of her.

'Hi.' I dumped my shopping on the chair opposite. 'I'll just get myself a coffee.'

Mrs Munroe gave a weak smile and taking up her fork piled a large piece of cake into her mouth.

Waiting to be served, I took a surreptitious glance across the room at Mrs Munroe. I felt sure she'd put on weight, quite a lot of it, since last I'd seen her. That was when she'd visited me in the hospital, about six months ago. I watched as another chunk of chocolate cake disappeared; that was definitely comfort eating so what's got her so depressed?

Sitting down opposite I smiled my most friendly smile. 'It's lovely to see you, Mrs Munroe, how are things?'

She finished eating, took a large gulp of her latte and very slightly shrugged her shoulders, turning her head to gaze out of the window. 'I miss her,' she said quietly.

'Who, Lily?'

Mrs Munroe gave a brief nod.

'But I thought you wanted her to go on the art course; Lily said you helped persuade her dad to let her go.'

'Yes, I did and I'm glad she's doing what she truly wants at last, goodness knows she's had to wait long enough to break free but…' Mrs Munroe paused, 'the house is *so empty.*'

I reached across and gently touched her hand, lying lifeless on the table still clutching the fork. 'I know, I miss her too; that was why I wanted to talk to you; partly for any ideas you could give me for her birthday gift and to find out if you knew how she is; she's not been in touch with me as much as she used to.'

'Oh, I expect she's just busy with her studies.' Mrs Munroe looked down at her empty plate, deliberately avoiding eye contact.

'Do you really think that's all it is?'

'Well, her life's very different now, isn't it? She's amongst a lot of people her own age, all with the same interests. I expect she's busy socialising.'

I felt a slight catch in my breathing and barely wanting to hear the answer, 'Is there someone in particular?'

Mrs Munroe started fidgeting with her paper napkin. 'I don't think so. She says she's just concentrating on her painting and needing time and space alone. Says she often goes for long drives and walks in the Scottish countryside; helps her mind to settle.'

'She's still got her little car then, a Skoda wasn't it; bright yellow with a black stripe? I remember I used to tease her about driving around in a wasp, but one that didn't have a sting in its tail!'

'Yes, she loves that car.' Mrs Munroe paused, considering. 'She's still trying to come to terms with everything that happened.'

'Isn't that a good thing?'

'Yes, of course it is. I'm just feeling sorry for myself. We were so close, did so much together and now there's just me and Eddie; it's such a huge gap.'

'Still, she'll be coming home for her birthday, won't she?'

'No, she messaged this morning; she's staying in Scotland, planning to do a long hike up Ben Carrick on her birthday. Says it's a personal challenge; if she can do that all by herself then she'll feel she's really getting somewhere with her overall recovery. I still worry about her, out there on her own but she insists she's fine; knows what she's doing. She's got all the proper gear.' Mrs Munroe picked up the fork and absent-mindedly stabbed its prongs into the paper napkin, tearing it to shreds. 'It'll just be me listening to Eddie banging on about his latest case.' She sighed again, her despair palpable. 'But what's new.'

Mrs Munroe's words swam around inside my head. I couldn't give a damn how unhappy she was except inasmuch as it probably meant that home life for DCI Eddie Munroe wasn't exactly a bed of roses either but I did care, very much, about Lily; I would have to get up to Scotland sooner than I'd thought.

CHAPTER 12

B ack at home that evening I had to acknowledge that Shirley Munroe's update on Lily had bothered me. Lily might be keeping very much to herself, finding solace in solitude and beautiful scenery but I couldn't risk her becoming too independent, getting stronger. It might make my task more difficult; the more fragile she was the easier she would be to overcome.

I poured myself a glass of Pinot Noir and settled on the window seat next to Liliad. 'Direct action is what's needed but I can't just up sticks and go to Scotland; I'll have to beg some holiday from work and arrange a B & B a distance from the art school.' I reached across to the coffee table and picked up my laptop. Settling it on my lap I looked at Liliad as I expressed my thoughts out loud. 'I don't want to let Lily know my intentions in advance as she'll probably try to put me off but if I just turn up it'll be much more difficult for her to be dismissive. I can use the excuse I wanted to surprise her for her birthday. Fortunately that's at least two weeks away as I can't see Robyn allowing any less notice of leave than that. In the meantime I can find out if my anonymous gifts to our Miss Melissa Hartnell have had the desired effect.' Chuckling at the thought I poured another glass of wine and settled down to my research.

The following weekend I drove into town, leaving my car in the car park next to the theatre and walked the short distance to Cadogan Square. I needed to manufacture a meeting with Melissa, make her acquaintance and start to gain her trust. Obviously she was bound to tell Dr Metcalfe about me at some point so I knew I'd have to disguise my appearance. Nothing particularly dramatic, just enough to muddy the waters and leave room for doubt.

Changing one's looks is so easy these days. I donned a brown wig of shoulder-length hair, a calf-length A-line skirt and tailored jacket completely out of character to what I normally wear which is jeans and T-shirt or smart trousers and shirt blouse for work. I painted my nails bright red and wore silver pendant earrings. In contrast to my usual understated makeup I ensured that my eyes were a noticeable feature behind the large, round lenses of designer specs.

It was a bit of a long shot but I was hoping, it being Saturday morning, that Melissa might go into the café on the corner of the Square for a coffee or, failing that, that I'd be able to see if she left her apartment.

The café was pretty busy, definitely a meeting place for friends as the waitress had stated. Serving behind the counter was the same woman I'd chatted to on my earlier visit but she obviously didn't recognise me at all which was encouraging. I ordered an Americano with hot milk; it's important not to leave any trails of similarity and settled down by the window once more to wait. Now that I knew Melissa's apartment was central and at the front of the building, I could see that her blinds were pulled back letting in the winter sunshine so could assume that at least she was up and about.

I'd taken a magazine with me to flick through whilst I waited coming across an absorbing article on a new exhibition at the London Portrait Gallery and became so distracted I almost missed Melissa walking briskly in the direction of town. Damn! I'd hoped she'd call into the café but no luck. I'd have to follow her and hope to engineer an accidental encounter.

Hastily, I gathered up my things, thanked the waitress and stepped outside just in time to see Melissa turn the corner. I reached the corner about three minutes after her. It was a fairly straight road that led into the heart of the town and I just spotted her as she turned left toward the Mall. Entering she headed straight up the escalator toward the train station which panicked me for a moment but, thank goodness she stopped at the coffee shop. I wandered past a little way, calling into the health food shop for a non-committal browse but all the time keeping an eye on Melissa. The coffee shop had tables in an area of the Mall just outside its open plan frontage. Melissa settled herself at one of these tables, looking toward the escalator.

Quickly I bought a couple of items and strolled back toward the coffee shop intending to take a table directly next to Melissa and strike up a conversation but at that moment I saw her raise a hand in greeting as Dr Metcalfe stepped off the escalator. They briefly hugged and Melissa joined the queue for coffee, leaving Dr Metcalfe seated at their table so I too joined the queue and fell in behind her. She seemed slightly on edge, nervously fiddling with a loose strand of hair as we waited. Having bought a couple of black coffees she returned to join Dr Metcalfe. I completed my purchase and chose a seat two tables away from where I could observe and judge the atmosphere between them and hopefully overhear some of their conversation.

For a couple about to be married in September they didn't seem particularly happy. Dr Metcalfe's expression was stern, almost sour and Melissa, by her tone and body language, appeared to be placatory. Dr Metcalfe said something I couldn't catch but Melissa, her voice slightly raised was almost pleading.

'But I *don't know* who's been sending them; I thought it was you. Why would I even tell you about them if I knew it wasn't you but someone else? I'd want to keep it a secret, wouldn't I? Please, Andrew be reasonable.'

'Someone at work, is it? That new teacher you told me about recently. You talked about him quite a lot when he first arrived; breath of fresh air you said. Is it him?'

'No! I'm sure it isn't. He'd have no reason and anyway, he's married.'

Dr Metcalfe gave a petulant shrug. 'I don't see that as a barrier.'

Melissa sighed, 'Please, Andrew, can we just forget about it. This is meant to be an enjoyable day; we're meant to be booking our honeymoon.'

Dr Metcalfe gave a slight nod of acknowledgement, reaching across the table and taking hold of Melissa's hand. 'I'm sorry; I just get so jealous when I think of anyone else wanting you. I couldn't bear to lose you.'

'Oh, Andrew you won't lose me. I swear there's no-one else. Perhaps those things were put outside the wrong door; there was no note of any kind attached.'

'Yes, you're right; probably just some stupid delivery boy's mistake. Come on, drink up and we'll go and book our honeymoon.'

I sat where I was for a couple of minutes, mentally hugging myself at the success of my efforts. Seeds of doubt had obviously been sown in Dr Metcalfe's mind even if he was making an effort to shrug them off. I watched the couple take the escalator down to the ground floor of the Mall and was able to see them enter the travel agents. They'd probably be in there for quite some time so I decided to buy myself a sandwich and another coffee. Returning to the same table I settled down to enjoy my lunch, all the time keeping the travel agents in view. It was worth hanging on as I really wanted to keep things moving forward; to meet up with Melissa and make her acquaintance especially as I was planning my trip to Scotland and would be away for, I hoped, about a week.

I'd finished my lunch and had been waiting for a further half hour before they came out of the travel agents. What on earth had they been organising? A world cruise! Hurrying down the escalator I caught up with them just as they reached the main doors. Now all smiles and affection they hugged and kissed before Dr Metcalfe turned toward the multi-storey car park and Melissa headed up the High Street. In that direction she obviously wasn't going straight home so I kept following.

Eventually she turned into the Manor Lane Amateur Theatre building. I hesitated in the forecourt; I'd never been here before and there was obviously no performance happening as it was late morning so what was she doing there and what excuse could I find for going inside? I hovered for a while, uncertain of my next move when I spotted a container of leaflets affixed to the wall. Taking one out I found it gave details of upcoming performances but also contained a section on membership and volunteering. Just what I needed; I pushed open the door and stepped inside.

The foyer was quite small but pleasantly carpeted and decorated. A cubbyhole of a ticket office was just inside the door and the walls of the foyer were decorated with framed photographs of numerous productions. In the far corner was a counter with cups and saucers laid out in neat rows, a sink, fridge, kettle indicating that this was the coffee and tea area. To my right, down a couple of steps, an open door led into a bar area; again small but very cosy, presumably for pre-performance drinks and gatherings.

There didn't seem to be anyone about so I just kept going. A narrow corridor stretched before me as I took a few tentative steps in that direction. Pulling aside a door curtain I found the theatre itself; the auditorium furnished with comfortable, raked seating. This was clearly a serious amateur dramatic company.

Continuing down the corridor I came to a closed door baring my way. I hesitated, not sure whether to proceed until I just caught the sound of voices and laughter. Slightly nervously I knocked and turned the handle. The room opened out into a large area with tables strewn with multi-coloured costumes. Three women sat busily working; mending and altering garments as they chatted.

A plump lady, dressed in loose fitting trousers and a smock looked up as I entered. 'Can I help?'

I glanced around the room but Melissa wasn't there. 'I'm sorry to trouble you but I was wondering about joining as a volunteer and was hoping I could get some more information but I couldn't find anyone to ask. I've picked up a leaflet.' I held up the pamphlet as evidence of my serious intentions.

A woman busily hemming a gorgeous Regency looking costume suggested, 'You need to fill out the application form and send it in to the address on the leaflet, indicating what you might be interested in.'

'That's the trouble, I don't really know; it's why I'd hoped to talk with someone.'

'Well, there's not anyone here who can help at present,' the plump lady replied, 'you'd do better to do as Rose suggested. Fill in the form as best you can and put a little note with it explaining. Our membership secretary will then get in touch and might arrange a few sessions with the other volunteers; that way you'll be able to find out what you like best.'

I realised I wasn't going to get anywhere so smiled sweetly and left. 'Sod it!' I turned and thumped my fist against the entrance door as it slammed behind me. God knew where Melissa had disappeared to but I could only assume that she was a volunteer, otherwise what reason could she have for going in there. I'd have to take a chance but if I got myself entangled in this and she wasn't involved I would definitely be kicking the neighbour's cat!

Heading back to my car in the main shopping car park I realised with some dismay that I'd been hours, much longer than I'd originally intended; the car park charge was going to be huge!

CHAPTER 13

L iliad was sitting on the window seat gazing out toward the roofline of St Joseph's when I got home. Strange, I was sure I'd deliberately left her facing into the room away from the window.

I went straight to the bedroom to change out of my outfit and remove the wig and heavy eye make-up feeling dejected at what I'd failed to achieve. I was also worrying about the lack of contact with Lily; she was the pawn in the game to devastate DCI Munroe so I couldn't risk her getting away from me.

I settled down next to Liliad on the window seat and went over what had happened during the day. 'Dr Metcalfe's definitely got the hump over the flowers and chocs I left outside Melissa's. He doesn't seem to be very trusting, which is an odd way to feel about someone you're planning to spend the rest of your life with, although

Melissa seems a total innocent, quite ingenuous. I think she volunteers at the local amateur theatre so I'm going to have to get myself in there as well. It's the only way I can think of to hopefully make a friendship without arousing any suspicion.'

Next day I filled out the form, giving my name as Joanne (Jo) Simons and sent it off first class; I could only hope their membership secretary wouldn't be tardy.

On the Lily front I'd found a B & B about thirty miles from the art school and booked my train ticket; I'd hire a car once up there. Now all I had to do was persuade Robyn to give me time off work. I broached the subject first thing on Monday morning.

'When were you thinking of going?' Robyn asked; a note of concern evident.

'In a couple of weeks; it's my cousin's birthday; a big family party.'

Robyn's face fell. 'Look, Annalee I'm not trying to be awkward but that week is really busy. I don't know if you've looked at the calendar but it's the week of two major symposiums. I really can't afford to be short staffed.'

'I'm sorry but it's considered really important in my family to be at these things; perhaps if I didn't take the whole week, just two or three days.' I pleaded.

Robyn hesitated. 'OK, but we'll have to get everything in place before you leave so you're going to have to pull out all the stops over the next couple of weeks.'

'Thanks, Robyn; I really appreciate it.'

The next two weeks were so pressured at work I really didn't need to be bothered with the theatre company even though I knew it was important to keep up the momentum as regards Melissa and Dr Metcalfe. In the event, the company's membership secretary rang me during the first week, on the Wednesday evening.

'Thanks for your application and I do understand the difficulty. I wondered if you'd like to come along Friday evening, meet some of the members and chat about the different aspects of putting on a production, to help you make up your mind. We're in the middle of rehearsals at the moment for Lady Windermere's Fan so most of the cast and technicians will be there especially as Friday evenings are also social gatherings once rehearsals are over, so it's quite informal.'

I knew I'd be knackered by Friday evening but didn't dare miss this opportunity so only hesitated briefly. 'Yes, that'd be fine; about what time?'

'Say about seven; my name's Maggie, I'll look out for you.'

'Great; see you Friday then.' Putting down the phone I muttered to myself, 'Oh, God, that's going to be really tight. I'll need to have my meal at work lunch time 'cos I'll never get back in time to eat plus change my appearance and get over to the theatre by seven. Oh, why does everything have to happen at once?'

◆

Friday evening came round with alarming speed, the week simply flying past. Robyn had been right, the two symposiums required a huge amount of preparation, so much so that I'd already worked a couple of hours overtime on Monday and Tuesday and it was looking as though the following week was going to follow the same pattern.

Nevertheless I'd managed to leave Friday only half an hour later than normal; dashed home, made up my face, settled the wig and dressed in smart but casual trousers and a slightly flouncy blouse. I was in such a hurry I'd got half way down the stairs when I realised I'd forgotten my designer specs. Dashing back up, I barely glanced at Liliad in her usual place on the window seat. As I sped out the door I had the vague impression that she was sitting particularly close to the edge of the seat but I didn't have time to fuss over that now.

Running down the stairs I flung open the front door and practically cannonballed into Carol, my downstairs flatmate, who was on her way in. Muttering a brief apology I put my head down and turned away from her. I felt her eyes boring into my back as I hurried down the path and almost made the mistake of getting into my own car! I could sense her confusion; that I seemed familiar but at the same time didn't and realised, in the same instance, that I'd automatically applied my usual perfume. Oh, Annalee, stupid, stupid mistake! Many people use the same perfume, I know but any connections can trigger doubt and suspicion. As it was, I had to lose more time walking down the road, taking out my mobile and calling for a taxi. I hadn't intended to take a cab but on reflection it probably was wiser not to let anyone at the theatre see my car.

Arriving ten minutes late I made my apologies to Maggie, claiming the taxi firm had let me down.

'Not to worry, not everyone's here yet. Let me show you round the building first and then we'll discuss some of the volunteering options we have at the moment.'

An hour later we'd finished the tour and I'd been introduced to a number of people, all obviously talented in the various aspects of putting on a polished production and I was feeling more and more out of my depth, wondering what on earth I could offer and *still* I hadn't seen Melissa. Agitation was increasing making it difficult for me to pay full attention to what Maggie and others were saying. Every time a door opened I'd glance that way hoping it would be Melissa; I must have given the impression of being extremely rude considering the trouble Maggie was going to but she was too polite to comment.

Eventually we made our way back to the bar area, Maggie pointing out that bar staff and front of house people were always needed and I was finding it increasingly difficult not to commit myself to at least *something* when, at last, Melissa walked in, went straight up to the bar and asked for a large G and T.

Clutching her drink she turned, leant against the counter and perused the room, catching Maggie's eye as she did so.

'Mel, let me introduce Jo; she's considering joining our happy throng but she's having difficulty deciding just what she wants to do. You could do with some help in make-up couldn't you, especially as we'll need cover when you're off on your honeymoon in September?' Maggie turned to me, 'Are you any good at doing make-up, Jo; do you think that might interest you?'

Relief washed over me, not only because Melissa had at last turned up but because I knew make-up was one area I could genuinely manage. 'Well, I've always liked experimenting with make-up although I don't know much about stage make-up; I'd love to learn though.' I smiled at Melissa who was nodding her head slowly, as though considering.

'I could do with a hand, it's true and I will be away for a while later in the year. I did have some help from Denise if you remember, Maggie but she's due to have her first child soon so she's going to be tied up with that.' She addressed me directly, 'Are you free this Sunday afternoon, about three? Our next production is Lady Windermere's Fan so nothing too extreme to start with. You can see how you get on making me up as Lady Windermere and we'll take it from there if you'd like.'

'I'll give it a go, definitely.'

'Great, see you here then.' With that, Melissa walked across to join a table of five others, from the greetings well known friends. I realised I couldn't possibly intrude, I'd have to wait until Sunday when I was alone with her to start forming a friendship so I turned to Maggie, expressing my thanks for all her help and offering to buy her a drink.

After my busy week at work by ten thirty I was feeling absolutely knackered so made my excuses to leave the group I'd been sitting with. The cold night air was like a slap in the face as I stepped out into the theatre forecourt, waking me up after the warm fug of the bar and the couple of drinks I'd had. As I hadn't got my car I knew I'd have to walk into town to the taxi rank.

I was always alert to my surroundings, especially at night, so I quickly became aware of a shadowy figure standing amongst the bushes that formed the left hand boundary of the forecourt. It was definitely a man, not particularly tall but solid framed and standing absolutely still. At that instant a car drove past on the road and for a second its headlights arced across the static figure, briefly illuminating his dark overcoat which hung open revealing a flash of red silk lining to the suit jacket underneath as he swiftly turned and moved away from me.

Walking into town I kept casting my eyes about me but was soon convinced, whoever he was, he wasn't following me and decided it probably was just someone's partner waiting to take them home. I'd learnt that they closed the bar at eleven so it seemed a reasonable assumption.

I got a taxi with no difficulty but made him drop me a few yards from the house. Having bumped into Carol on my way out I didn't want to risk her seeing me return and walking up the front path to let myself in as she'd naturally be suspicious of someone she'd seen earlier but didn't recognise letting themselves into my flat. Instead I walked briskly past our front entrance gate, down the side of the garden and pushed my way through a thin section of hedge close to the building, well out of range of any of Carol's front windows. Holding my breath, I let myself in as quietly as I could and hurried up the stairs.

When I entered my flat I didn't go immediately into the lounge as I normally do but went straight to the bed-room, desperate to remove my wig which was irritating my scalp to the point of screaming. I tore it off, flinging it on the bed and frantically scratched at my short hair that lay flattened to my head like a skull cap. I decided, it being so late, I might as well remove all the heavy make-up too so sauntered through into the bathroom. Face cleansed I then ran a bath, wanting to relax and revisit all that had happened during the evening.

After my soak, I wandered through into the kitchen and made a night cap. Consequently I must have been home for at least an hour and a half before I went into the lounge to relate everything to Liliad and so clarify things in my own mind.

I started talking as I entered the room without really looking. 'It was worth my going; Melissa was there … eventually and …' I stopped in my tracks, shock strangling my words as I stared, transfixed at the empty window seat. The cushion Liliad always leant against was in place,

I could see the faint indented outline of her body, but she wasn't there.

'Liliad,' I called again, 'Liliad, where are you?'

I could feel panic rising as I hurried up to the seat, stupidly picking up the cushion as though I'd find her hiding behind it. Slinging the cushion back down I turned, frantically scanning the room. As I took a step forward my toe collided with something on the floor. Instinctively I glanced down; it was one of Liliad's black shoes! Horrified I sank to my knees, craning my head to look under my sofa and armchair, picking up the shoe as I did so. It was then I caught sight of a tiny stockinged foot peeping out from under the sofa.

I scurried across the floor on my hands and knees and gently pulled Liliad out from underneath. She was coated in dust and fluff (I felt an irrational pang of shame at my lack of housekeeping) and cradled her on my lap as I gently tried to untangle her strings. It was as though someone had been trying to make a cat's cradle of them, they were so entwined.

'Oh, Liliad what's happened? How on earth did you get under there and … where's your other shoe?'

I pushed my hand under the sofa, feeling along for the second shoe. 'Ouch!' A sharp pain shot through my hand. I instinctively drew it back. Three long scratches began to seep blood, suddenly next door's cat streaked past me and out onto the landing.

Tumbling backwards in shock, my heart thumping and my breath coming in ragged gulps I took a few seconds to gather my wits. Laying Liliad gently on the floor I went out onto the landing. Fortunately I'd closed the doors into my other rooms; the cat had nowhere else to go but down the stairs. I leant over the landing bannisters. He was hunched up against the closed bottom door.

Slowly I walked down, the cat's eyes and mine locked in mutual hatred. He pressed himself tightly into the corner by the door hinges as I descended. I stopped on the bottom step and reached across, pushing the door open as I undid the latch.

As soon as it opened a fraction the cat shot out. I hurried after him and swiftly opened the front door so he could make his escape into the garden. As he raced past me I kicked out, managing to land a satisfying whack on his backside.

Hurrying back upstairs, I gently lifted Liliad up onto the window seat, and spent some time carefully untying the knots from her strings and hiding them once again behind her cushion. 'Oh, Liliad I'm so sorry. He must have somehow got into the downstairs lobby and followed me up when I suddenly realised I'd forgotten my specs and came back up to get them. I must have left the bottom door open.'

I could feel the tears starting as I gently turned Liliad's head toward me but for some reason her head wouldn't stay there; it kept turning slowly away from me. I couldn't make out why; there didn't seem to be any physical damage other than a few scratches on her legs and arms.

As I sat sadly contemplating Liliad and what my carelessness had resulted in, I felt so fatigued; an exhaustion that I could no longer fight. I tucked a small blanket carefully around her and took myself off to bed, absent-mindedly picking at the razor cut scars on my arms.

CHAPTER 14

I woke late Saturday morning, despite the extra hours still feeling unnaturally fatigued; the trauma of the night before racing into my brain within a few seconds of waking. I felt physically sick as I recalled the empty window seat and Liliad's tiny, fragile body underneath the sofa.

She had become so precious to me over the years since I'd bought her but I only realised how much she meant when I thought I might have lost her. She understood me, I knew that without doubt every time I looked into her eyes and saw my own reflection three fathoms deep. She had a presence that sometimes chilled, sometimes comforted me and I knew I would be lost without her. I didn't know who had made her but whoever it was they had crafted something so much more than the wood and strings of which she consisted.

She'd had a terrible experience and goodness knows how long she'd been subjected to the cat's unwanted attention. Why oh why hadn't I gone into the lounge straight away as I normally did; she would have heard me come in and yet I'd simply prolonged her agony.

I wrapped my dressing gown around me and walked out onto the landing allowing myself a slight smile at the memory of my foot making contact with the cat's rear end as he made his escape.

Entering the lounge I could tell Liliad had hardly moved during the night, the blanket still securely tucked up under her chin. She didn't seem to be awake so I tiptoed back to my kitchen diner and made an instant coffee and some toast.

Standing eating at the window, I gazed down into the back garden just as next door's cat was venturing out onto our lawn. Immediately I rapped my knuckles against the glass. He froze, a front paw raised in anticipation of his next step and turned to look up in the direction of sound. I sensed his recognition and hesitancy. He knew I was no immediate threat where I was; his stare a direct challenge. Infuriated I flung open the window and yelled, 'SOD OFF!' That did the trick, surprised at the volume and vehemence in my voice he turned on the spot and jumped back over the fence. I closed the window, smirking with triumph.

Back in the lounge I sat beside Liliad and gently nudged her arm. The movement caused her to open her eyes but she turned away almost immediately and I felt a chill run through me, 'I've got to go back to the theatre tomorrow afternoon to have a go at being a make-up artist. It's my only real opportunity to form a friendship with Melissa. I hope you don't mind my leaving you alone again but I don't feel there's much choice. I'll make sure all the doors and windows are locked.'

The response was a cold stare.

◆

Sunday afternoon I presented myself at the theatre, careful to be on time so as to start off on a relaxed footing. Melissa was already there, laying out various make-up paraphernalia at one of the stations.

'Great, you're here. Before we start let me show you the costume and wig Lady Windermere will be wearing so you get an idea of period and colour scheme.'

We walked through into the wardrobe area; the place was crammed with costumes but Melissa went straight to a rack on the left of the room. 'These are the main costumes already set aside for this production.' She pulled out a beautiful dress in pale lilac and indicated a blonde wig on a dummy head. 'Do these give you some idea?'

'Mmm, think so.'

'OK, let's get started.'

I delved into my handbag and extracted a pair of thin, white gloves. Noticing Melissa's frown I explained, 'I'm sorry, it's nothing to worry about really but my skin can react to certain substances in the make-up; I promise it's not contagious.'

'No problem, better safe than sorry I suppose; you know best.'

In view of my intentions for the future I didn't want to leave any fingerprints back stage. Front of house didn't matter as trying to isolate one set from all the hundreds that must be out there would be a herculean task and in any case, I'd simply say I came to performances.

Forty five minutes later Melissa studied her reflection. 'Tell you what, just get that wig I pointed out to you, please.' Melissa settled it on her head and gave a few tweaks to some lose strands. 'Well, Jo, I'm impressed; for a first go at stage make-up you've done really well. I feel quite beautiful. You'll have to speed up a bit but that'll come with practice so don't fret over that. So, what do you think? Would you like to come on board?'

'Oh yes, I'd love to; thanks so much, Melissa.'

'Call me Mel, everyone does. Come on, hopefully the bar will be open; I'll get you a drink, you deserve it.'

As we sat sipping wine I ventured, 'Did I hear that you're getting married later in the year?'

'Yes, that's right; September.'

'Congratulations! I imagine you must be busy with all the plans.'

'Yes, it is getting a bit hectic and you know what it's like, it's all down to me, Andrew doesn't want to know; says he'll just turn up on the day.'

'Oh, that's a bit mean.'

Mel shrugged. 'He's a very busy man and I think he'd really rather have a simple, quiet 'do' with just close family but I'm afraid my parents have other ideas for their only child. They want to send me off in style.' She gave a half-hearted grin.

'What does your fiancé do?'

'He's a doctor, a consultant psychiatrist.'

It was my turn to be flippant. 'So who better to under-stand all the different emotions involved in your big day?'

Mel giggled, 'Very true, Jo. I will point that out to him next time he complains.'

We finished our drinks and parted company, making arrangements for me to turn up at the dress rehearsal in a couple of weeks' time to assist.

That was perfect as I would be back from Scotland by then.

CHAPTER 15

The following week sped by at work but by its end everything was as ready as it could be for the two symposiums; any temp that Robyn got in to cover my absence would have a really easy time.

'Annalee, you've earned your leave!' Robyn gave me a brief, friendly hug of gratitude, 'Thank you *so* much for all your efforts. Enjoy the break.'

I'd been careful not to tell Robyn where I was going; I wanted no chance of a connection being made between myself and Scotland and therefore, by inference, Lily.

Driving home I could feel my anticipation mounting, I really was looking forward to the trip, the chance to see some of Scotland. I'd had so few holidays over the years it felt like a real adventure.

I'd been slowly putting things together for the trip during the week so only had the final items to pack. Once everything was done I made myself have an early night ready for the long journey.

Next day I was up early, had breakfast and settled Liliad well back on the window seat, a soft blanket wrapped around her in case the nights turned chilly. 'I've left the central heating on low so you should be fine and I'll make sure everything is securely locked so you won't have to worry about next door's cat making another unwelcome visit! I'm sorry I can't take you with me but I feel this is something I need to do on my own, especially after what happened to you last time.' I leant forward and placed a gentle kiss on her forehead, then turned and left without a backward glance.

I found the train journey up to Inverness blissfully relaxing; the stunning scenery and soporific motion of the train almost causing me to forget my purpose. I'd bought my train tickets with cash and found a small B & B within walking distance of the station where I also intended to pay by cash so there would be no card transactions to allow a trace of my movements; also, no taxi driver to remember me.

I'd had a lengthy chat with the landlady of the B & B when I'd booked and ascertained that she wasn't in the least averse to being paid in cash, no questions asked so I ventured to enquire if she knew a local second hand car dealer who'd be prepared to conduct business in the same manner; she'd been extremely helpful.

After a good night's sleep and a hearty breakfast I followed my landlady's directions to McFaddens Auto Dealers and acquired a respectable looking Vauxhall that I was assured was 'a nice little runner' for cash and no questions asked.

I spent the rest of that day driving around Inverness and surrounding areas to be sure I hadn't been sold a complete 'pup' which, despite my cynicism, I found I hadn't. Another night's rest and I was eager to move on.

I knew from my conversation with Mrs Munroe that Lily was intending to walk up Ben Carrick on her birthday so it was imperative that I was there on that day. I'd booked a B & B about thirty miles from where Lily was based at the Art Centre. A cash deal again under a false name and far enough away from the Art Centre for no association. I also made a point of joking with the landlady about my lack of inclination for exercise, making sure all my hiking gear was hidden away in the car boot.

I knew there was a car park at the start of the Ben Carrick hike and that Lily would be sure to start from there, everybody did. This was ideal as I didn't want to meet her at the Art Centre; too much chance of being seen together. I had to acknowledge that my plan was a bit of a long shot as although Lily had told Mrs Munroe she intended to walk alone there was always the chance that she'd change her mind and have someone with her but I decided to be philosophical about that; even if it did happen at least I'd have had a good holiday in Scotland, somewhere I'd always wanted to go and I'd simply have to re-think and re-plan. I was nothing if not patient.

'So, where are you off to today then? Doing any walking?' The landlady was the nosey sort so I thought I'd give her enough information to satisfy her curiosity but not enough to be of any use.

'Me, walking? You must be joking. Have car will travel is my motto. I'm heading south. Thanks for the breakfast; I'm sorry it's only the one night.'

'Where are you booked into next?'

'I'm not; I'll just find somewhere when I've done enough driving; I think 'pot luck' is more fun!'

She looked doubtful. 'Rather you than me; I need everything well planned out or I'm a nervous wreck.'

'Really? I've slept in the car before now! Anyway, I must be off; thanks again.'

'Bye lassie; have a safe journey.'

I picked up my overnight bag and made my escape. I was lucky, the weather was dry and quite clear so nothing in the elements to put Lily off her planned hike.

It took me about an hour to reach the car park at the foot of Ben Carrick. There was one other car, devoid of occupants, but it wasn't Lily's. I was glad I'd casually checked that with Mrs Munroe. I didn't have to worry about Lily noticing my car, it being a hire and nothing she was familiar with. I'd changed into my walking gear in a layby en route so walked a little way from the car park and hid behind some large boulders but from a point where the car park was still visible. Hopefully, I shouldn't have to wait too long. It was still relatively early in the year so the light didn't last long enough for tardy starts. If Lily was going to do this walk she needed to be here by nine thirty at the latest.

Nine o'clock and Lily's little Skoda pulled into the car park. I watched as she donned her walking boots and padded, waterproof jacket. Mrs Munroe was right, Lily did have all the gear but I couldn't help noticing how pale and frail she looked despite obviously believing she had the stamina to tackle the climb. It was clear she had a long way to go before she had regained the weight and confidence she'd had before the shooting but she was obviously trying. It was a shame her efforts were due to end so soon; I did have quite a fondness for Lily but one can't let sentiment stand in one's way; I reasoned that no-one truly wants to struggle through life so all in all I was doing her a favour.

All togged up, OS map checked and double checked, Lily set off. I let her get a good way ahead until it became clear that she planned to take the easier of the two routes to the summit. She wasn't striding out particularly fast, presumably pacing herself and conserving her energy for later. It was clear that I'd have no difficulty catching her up when I chose especially if she stopped to take photographs; I'd noticed the camera around her neck.

We'd been walking about an hour when Lily stopped for water and some photos. This was my opportunity; I speeded up coming up behind her. She wasn't aware of my presence; the wind was strong emitting a whining roar which smothered the sound of my boots on the rocky terrain and she was totally absorbed in the photographs she was capturing.

'Oh my God; Lily! How weird is this?'

If the strap had not been around her neck the camera would have shattered on the rocks at her feet.

'Annalee?' Shock froze on her face, my name spat out like spittle, her mouth agape with confusion and disbelief.

I grinned at her. 'How much of a coincidence is this? I didn't know you liked hiking.' I ploughed on, keeping the momentum going, not leaving Lily any gap in which to challenge me although she appeared too stunned to do so. 'I'm sure I told you I'd like to visit Scotland one day when you first told me about the Art Centre. Are you enjoying it there? It must be a fabulous place to learn about landscape painting. Is that what you're doing up here and with the photographs; getting some material for later?'

I paused for breath but Lily was still dumbfounded, as if her brain couldn't compute the reality of my presence. 'Shall we walk together the rest of the way? We can catch up on each other's news.' Gently I took hold of Lily's arm and turned her in the direction of the summit, propelling her forward as I walked on. She didn't resist, almost stupefied with shock and besides, what could she say or do? She had no valid reason for insisting on carrying on alone and in any case, it would be somewhat difficult to achieve as we were both on the same path. That, coupled with

Lily's innate sense of good manners left her no option but to stay with me.

We climbed on, me talking the whole time to a basically mute Lily. When she did venture to respond it was clear she was finding it difficult to talk and walk at the same time. I didn't help by keeping the pace fairly brisk, that coupled with the ever strengthening wind was proving a challenge for her. It seemed my initial assessment at the car park had been correct. All I now had to hope for was that no-one else would be at the summit when we reached it.

The final assent to the small summit plateau was short but steep and very rugged making it essential to concentrate where one was putting one's feet as it was so easy to roll on loose boulders. The last thing I needed was to slip myself – that would be ironic.

Lily was definitely struggling at this point so I held her arm to help steady her the final few feet. Once on the plateau we both stood for a few minutes, gathering our breath. I took a quick look to all sides but could see no-one else in view. Whoever had left their car in the car park had obviously been and gone by the alternative route.

I tapped Lily's arm and pointed East, having to raise my voice above the ever strengthening wind. 'Look over there; what a fabulous, desolate landscape especially with those dark clouds scudding across the sky. You ought to take a photo of that before the weather closes in.'

Lily nodded an acknowledgement and walked to the edge of the plateau, extracting her camera as she did so.

I knew that on that side the plateau ends abruptly, with the extremely steep ridge plummeting beyond with great walls of crags on each flank. The view is one of a vast wilderness.

As Lily neared the edge and raised the camera to her eye I took the few short steps that lay between us at a brisk trot, lurching forward as I came within reach, cannonballing into Lily's back.

It was over in a second although it seemed to play out in slow motion. I watched, fascinated as Lily seemed to turn in mid-air as she tumbled over the edge. She must have been turning back toward me at the point of impact. Disastrously I hadn't collided with her hard enough to propel her out, away from the edge. Instead she sort of slid over the drop, managing to grab onto the granite edge with one hand as she slipped, her feet dangling below with no ledge on which to secure her footing; her other hand grabbing at a small projection of crag further down.

I flung myself down on my front and grabbed hold of a wrist, attempting to pull her up. 'Lily, I can't pull you up on just one arm; I'm not strong enough. You've got to let go of the rock with your other hand so I can grab that. I can pull you up if I've got hold of both arms.'

Gripped in a paroxysm of terror and panic Lily shrieked, 'I can't; I daren't let go.'

'Lily, you've got to; you've got to trust me. I'll catch your hand, I promise. I won't let you fall. Please, Lily; *now*. I can't hold onto you like this much more.'

Lily hesitated a fraction longer, then let go of the crag with her left hand, reaching it upwards for me to grab. As she did so she looked straight into my eyes. In that split second I sensed she knew. I released my hold on her right wrist. She plummeted to her death in total silence.

I pushed myself up onto all fours, breathing in short gasps, as the enormity of what I'd done washed over me. It was exhilarating! At last, after all these years, I had my revenge on DCI Munroe. I'd proved that I was an 'irritation' he could not scratch away and what I had done would be with him for 'ever and ever, amen.' I could have skipped with delight.

I got to my feet, surveying the bleak landscape all around me, taking deep breaths of the cold air to steady myself for the long descent. The weather was closing in; I needed to make a move. I shifted my rucksack onto my back and turned toward my car and the next pawns in my game.

CHAPTER 16

I made good time back to Inverness, abandoning my car on a side street and walking the rest of the way to the railway station, catching the overnight sleeper back to London.

I found that, for the first time in months, I slept soundly rocked by the motion and background thrum of the train and the satisfying sense of achievement; of a job well done. It would be interesting to see how long it took for Lily to be missed. It being the Centre's break time *they* wouldn't miss her until the students returned and Mrs Munroe wasn't expecting her home as she knew she was planning the hike. I expect she might get concerned when she couldn't contact her daughter but she'd probably put it down to mobile phone problems; for a while at least.

By the time I arrived in London I felt quite refreshed and eager to get home to Liliad to tell her how well the game had panned out; that way I knew I could revisit events and enjoy the sensation all over again. The re-telling would also help cement everything in my mind; I didn't want to lose one minute of the adventure.

Good fortune seemed to be with me; my local train pulled in on time and I was home by nine o'clock on a sunny, warm morning. I went straight into the lounge, determined not to make Liliad wait a moment longer on her own. Opening the door, the room smelt slightly fusty having been shut up for a few days but otherwise all seemed in order. Liliad was still on the window seat where I'd left her although the blanket I'd wrapped around her had slipped and was now only covering her legs. Also, she was turned to face the window, looking out at St Joseph's. That was strange; I was sure I'd left her facing into the room but perhaps I was mistaken; so much had been happening lately.

Throwing my backpack and luggage onto the sofa I plonked onto the window seat beside Liliad, picking her up and placing her on my lap to face me. 'It's over; I've done it!'

Liliad's eyes stared back at me, her pupils bigger and blacker than ever. As I stared at my reflection in her eyes I once again had the weird sensation of being sucked down into their depths, like sinking into a viscous bog; suffocating.

I squeezed my eyes tight and shook my head to rid myself of the feeling and when I looked again there was nothing, just Liliad's enchanting gaze. 'I think I'll have a cup of tea and a couple of biscuits,' I told her as I set her back on the seat, 'I'm feeling a bit light-headed, I think my sugar levels must be low; it's been quite a while since I've eaten.'

As I dropped the tea bag into the kitchen waste bin I noticed the shrivelled remains of the freesias Lily had given me on her final visit. I felt nothing.

◈

I took another day off work to recuperate and went in on the Friday which earned me some brownie points with Robyn. It was important for me to retain this job; it was easy but interesting and I really didn't want any upheaval. I felt settled in my apartment and in the job. If those basics were ticking along nicely there was nothing to distract me from the games I liked to play and there was still much to accomplish.

In another week I was due to be at the Manor Road Theatre doing my first proper stint as a trainee make-up artist with Melissa. That was my opportunity to find out how things were between herself and Dr Metcalfe and for me to consolidate our acquaintance into a firm friendship.

The week sped by; Robyn was glad to have me back which was gratifying.

'How was the holiday?'

'Great thanks; I managed to fit in a few art exhibitions plus some trips to the coast.'

'Where was it you went?' Robyn flung the question over her shoulder as she hurried back to her office to answer the phone. 'I don't think you said.'

'I think I did,' I replied, 'I'll get us a coffee.'

Robyn held up a thumb in agreement as I made my way to the canteen, having deflected her question hopefully she'll have forgotten about it by the time I return.

The Friday evening I made sure I left work on time so that I didn't have to rush my change of appearance. It was a pain having to adopt the disguise for each time I was with Melissa but there was no way around it that I could see. The last thing I needed was for Dr Metcalfe to get wind of my presence.

I made sure I arrived at the theatre in good time to help Melissa with setting everything out. She was pleased to see me but nonetheless seemed a little down. Once the performance started and we had a few minutes to ourselves I asked if everything was alright.

'Yes I'm fine thanks, Jo; just got a lot on my mind.'

'Of course, your upcoming wedding; are the plans going well?'

'Yeah, not bad.' For someone planning what was meant to be the most important day of her life, Melissa didn't seem particularly enthusiastic. She sighed and sank heavily onto a chair at one of the make-up stations. I took the chair opposite and leant slightly toward her.

'Forgive me for asking but are you *sure* you're OK. I know you've not known me for long but if you'd like to talk, I'm a good listener.' I smiled encouragingly, 'it won't go any further, I promise; scouts honour!' I licked my finger and stuck it in the air. Melissa managed a brief chuckle.

'Oh, I'm not worried about that, just didn't want to bore you. I'll be fine; probably just hormones; as Andrew is fond of telling me.' Her tone sounded very slightly bitter. Fiddling with the jars on the table she continued, 'we'd better hang around here until the interval just in case anyone needs a touch up.'

To pass the time I settled myself at one of the stage side entrances to watch the show. These amateur actors really were very good; I could feel the bug beginning to bite and had to check myself. I had more important matters to pursue.

There was only a little bit of repair work to do at the interval; Melissa and I spent a few minutes putting items away, leaving performers to remove their own make up, so we made our way through to the bar for a well-earned drink.

'Andrew! What are you doing here?' Melissa, obviously surprised, seemed slightly flustered for a moment with, I thought, just a slight hint of annoyance giving edginess to her tone. I hung back in the shadows; I hadn't anticipated this, which I should have done. I wanted out of there as soon as I could but as I edged toward the front door Melissa called across.

'Jo, come and meet Andrew, my fiancé.'

I had no choice but to do as she asked, keeping my head bowed as though shy I murmured a 'hello', hardly daring to catch Andrew Metcalfe's eye.

'Jo's helping me with the make-up; she'll fill in for me when we're away.'

I noticed Melissa didn't say 'on honeymoon' which seemed odd; I thought all brides-to-be were only too eager to advertise their upcoming event.

'Jo, how very nice to meet you.' Dr Metcalfe held out his hand which to ignore would only have been noticeably rude. Keeping my eyes averted I could nevertheless sense his intense appraisal as he kept hold of my hand. The silence grew as neither of us attempted to move. At this close proximity I was terrified he'd recognise me despite my disguise. We'd spent so very many hours closeted in his consulting room, some vestiges of me must surely remain to give him cause for doubt; for suspicion. Suddenly, he broke the silence, 'Can I get you ladies a drink?'

'G and T please; how about you, Jo?'

'No thanks; I really need to be going.'

'What, so soon?' Dr Metcalfe sounded slightly bemused. 'I was hoping to get to know you better; I like to get to know Melissa's friends; it's important don't you think when you're planning to spend your life with someone.' He wrapped a proprietorial arm around Melissa's waist, pulling her toward him; an action with which she didn't seem particularly comfortable.

'Some other time; I must go now, things to do.' Leaving no room for further objections I turned and made my escape. Stepping out into the night air I found I was breathing heavily, a slight shakiness to my steps as I headed out of the forecourt toward the town centre and the taxi rank.

Seeing Dr Metcalfe was an unwelcome encounter but, as I walked, I had the distinct impression that my own discomfort was as nothing compared to Melissa's. She didn't seem at all pleased that her fiancé was there, that he'd surprised her by turning up unannounced. There was something not quite right in that relationship.

Stepping out of the taxi I could see that my downstairs neighbour, Carol was still up. Light shone through the slight gap in her curtains and an intermittent flickering suggested she was watching a late night movie. Hurrying up the path to the front door with the intention of getting into my flat as swiftly as I could to avoid yet another unwanted encounter, I didn't notice next door's cat. Bolting across the path he slammed into my ankles. I stumbled forward, my yell mixing with his shrieked meow of terror as I landed on top of him. Spitting and clawing he wriggled free and ran, leaving me spread-eagled on the path.

I pushed myself onto my feet; I had to get out of there before Carol came to investigate the noise. I hobbled to the side of the building just as I saw Carol's curtains drawn back as she peered outside. I pressed myself against the wall, my heart thumping like it was being played by a manic bongo drummer. Slowly my breathing returned to normal, Carol obviously thought better of venturing out to investigate and I was able to sneak up to my flat unobserved.

Collapsing on the sofa I kicked off my shoes, rolling up my trouser legs to examine my bruised knees. 'That sodding cat! I'll swing for it one day, Liliad.'

CHAPTER 17

Halfway through the following week I'd just got home from work and was at the kitchen sink, washing out a beautiful rainbow trout that I'd bought fresh from the supermarket along with some oven chips and a salad, the latter to salve my conscience about the chips, when my doorbell rang with a persistence that didn't bode well.

I dried my hands and hurried down the stairs to find Mrs Munroe standing on my doorstep looking larger than ever, her face a puffy red wobbling jelly of agitation.

'Mrs Munroe!'

'Can I come in please, Annalee; I need to speak with you.'

'Well, I was just about to have my dinner; can't it wait until tomorrow? I could meet you in Sainsbury's café then if you'd like, on my way home.'

Mrs Munroe hesitated, obviously not used to asserting herself but took a deep breath and insisted. 'No, I need to speak with you now. It's important.'

I shrugged, 'OK, if it's that important you'd better come up.'

I turned and led the way up my stairs as Mrs Munroe struggled laboriously behind me to an accompaniment of creaks that were either her knees or my stairs protesting at the unaccustomed weight.

I directed Mrs Munroe to my sofa, settled myself in the armchair opposite and waited.

Mrs Munroe undid her coat and leant slightly forward, resting her forearms on her thighs, her large breasts suspended just above her lap as if their weight was threatening to pull her down into a crumpled heap on the floor.

Seeming to gather her determination together Mrs Munroe launched straight in. 'I'm really worried about Lily; we haven't heard from her for three days now and the Art Centre is on skeleton staff as it's their holiday break; just a caretaker in from what we can make out. They've checked her room but say there's no sign of her having been there for a while.'

I shrugged. 'Perhaps she's staying with some friends if the place has practically closed down. Isn't she answering her phone?'

'No, it's not receiving our calls; the battery must have run down. Have you heard from her?'

'No, I told you, she hasn't been in touch with me much lately. I think she's given me the push.' I almost giggled at the irony of what I'd unintentionally said.

Mrs Munroe was fidgeting with the hem of her skirt; her eyes moist with despair and fear. 'Well, thanks for your time; I thought it was worth asking if you knew anything more than us.'

'What will you do?'

'Eddie is making enquiries of the local police and they've agreed to instruct the mountain rescue service to make a search.'

I knew this was bound to happen but it was important that I pleaded ignorance of Lily's intentions. 'Mountain rescue; why?'

Mrs Munroe looked slightly surprised. 'I told you; she was planning to do the hike up Ben Carrick.'

'Did you? I don't remember that. Are you sure? Why on earth would she do that on her own? It's a bit risky isn't it?'

Confused Mrs Munroe continued, 'She said she was sure she'd be fine; she was going to do the easier ascent; she said it was more of a rugged walk than a hike or climb. I was sure I'd told you.'

I shook my head, 'No, you definitely didn't. I wouldn't forget a thing like that.'

'Oh, I must be mistaken then; I've been a bit lost lately.' She looked down at her lap, absently plucking at a loose thread in her skirt. I could tell she was turning things over in her mind, trying to recall our conversation in

Sainsbury's. It was best she didn't ponder for too long; I needed to move things on.

I stood up to indicate that I wanted her to leave. 'I apologise but I really need to see to my dinner. I'm sorry I can't help you anymore. I'll let you know immediately if I do hear anything.'

Mrs Munroe levered herself out of my low sofa with some difficulty. 'Thank you, Annalee. I'm sorry to have disturbed you.'

'No problem. I'm sure she'll be fine.' I placed a comforting hand on her arm and followed her down the stairs, locking the doors firmly behind her. Once more entering my lounge I grinned across at Liliad. 'That went pretty well, don't you think.'

Liliad didn't respond; her head turned once more to look out the window at St Joseph's.

Over the next couple of weeks things seemed to fall into a gentle routine with work going smoothly and my apartment cosy and secure. I'd had the landlord round to fix the draughty bay window which had helped reduce my heating bill although it didn't seem to have stopped Liliad constantly staring out the window. It didn't matter which way I positioned her on the seat, her head always turned in that direction. Maybe I was being silly; she probably wasn't *just* looking at St Joseph's; more likely she was simply watching what was going on in the street below. I was away so much what with work, the Scotland trip and now the amateur theatre, she was probably crushingly bored. I resolved that once my current game was completed I'd spend more time with her. In fact, as much as I liked my apartment and job I was leaning toward the idea of moving away; changing area to somewhere no-one knew us. The anonymity was appealing.

Speaking of the game, I must move forward. It was amazing how quickly time sped by; before I knew it Melissa and Dr Metcalfe's wedding day would be upon us. Things seemed to be going well with Melissa but I needed to get closer. Fortunately, we'd decided it was a good idea to exchange phone numbers in case one of us couldn't make it to the theatre one night. I picked up my mobile and dialled.

'Hi, Melissa, it's Jo.'

'Oh hi, Jo; is everything OK?'

'Yeah, fine thanks. I just wondered if you'd like to meet up at the weekend; I'd like to buy you lunch as a thank you for all your help and advice on stage make-up.'

There was a slight pause on the other end of the phone as Melissa tried to decide. 'That's kind but there's really no need.'

'I know but I'd like to. There's a nice little café on the edge of Cadogan Square that does really good organic based foods. Do you know it?'

'Definitely; it's right close to where I live.'

'Is it? That sounds ideal then; say twelve noon on Saturday?' I crossed my fingers and waited.

'Yes, why not, it'll be nice to have a girly chin wag for
a change. I'll see you there.'

'Great. Bye.'

I turned to Liliad. 'Next stage set up; it gets easier with
practice.' I couldn't prevent the self-congratulatory grin
that spread across my face.

CHAPTER 18

They've found her.

It was on the six o'clock national news. I was surprised at that; I thought it'd make the local news but not the national but it seems DCI Munroe has been making quite a name for himself recently, dealing with some high profile cases so I guess that's why the media consider the loss of his daughter of national interest.

As I expected, the mountain rescue team discovered her. I didn't think it would take long once they started looking as it was known she was walking up Ben Carrick, even the route she was taking.

The news programme showed photos of Ben Carrick along with a map of the route Lily had walked. I pointed it out to Liliad. 'Look, that's where I walked; I told you the scenery was stunning, didn't I.'

They had a chap from mountain rescue surmising about what could have happened. He seemed gently critical of anyone walking such routes totally alone which I suppose was fair comment.

The broadcast then turned to DCI Munroe; he looked thinner than I remembered him; gaunt and strained. Beside him Mrs Munroe, squat and fat, looked like one of those papier-maché Japanese dolls; the sort that keep rolling back up to an upright position when knocked down. Talk about Jack Sprat and his wife! The interviewer, trying to sound sympathetic but in fact merely trying to put DCI Munroe on the spot, asked, 'Did you know your daughter was planning to do the hike alone?'

Munroe stiffened, fighting to keep his face an expressionless mask. 'No, I did not. Had I have known I would have prevented it.' Stony-faced he looked down toward his wife as he spoke but Shirley Munroe kept her eyes fixed on the ground at her feet, her lips pressed together in a tight line, forcing herself, it seemed to me, to hold her tongue.

The interviewer continued. 'I believe your daughter was seriously injured in a police armed raid only last year, Inspector Munroe. Was she truly recovered enough to take on such a challenging hike, do you think?'

Munroe glared. 'Apparently not,' and turned to leave, closing the interview but Mrs Munroe seemed to "screw her courage to the sticking place" as Shakespeare would say and unexpectedly piped up.

'Lily knew what she was doing; she wasn't behaving irresponsibly. She'd made all the right preparations; got all the right gear. It was an important part of her recovery; she'd been building up to the challenge for weeks; she wouldn't have done it if she didn't think she was ready.

Something happened up there. It wasn't her fault; I know it wasn't.'

Munroe stared at his wife, shocked at her outburst. He put out a hand to take her arm but she jerked away the second he made contact.

'What do you think could have happened? Surely she just slipped; got too close to the edge.' The interviewer pressed on, regardless of Munroe's desperate attempt to call a halt.

Shirley raised her head and looked directly at the camera. 'My daughter was an intelligent, sensible and cautious young woman. I do not believe this was an accident; I believe there was some incident; some unexpected happening up on that mountain that she couldn't possibly have prepared herself for and I won't rest until I find out what that was. That's all I have to say.' She turned away, slumped once more into herself; a roly-poly barrel of a woman.

I turned the television off and sat staring at the blank screen for several minutes. I hadn't thought that anyone would find Lily's fall suspicious; I'd counted on it being viewed as nothing more than a tragic accident as had happened on that very plateau a year previous when a man had slipped and tumbled to his death but Mrs Munroe's conviction disturbed me somewhat.

I went over everything in my mind. No, there was nothing incriminating; nothing that could connect me; I'd taken every precaution. Mrs Munroe could be as convinced as she pleased; it wouldn't get her anywhere.

I wandered into my kitchen and poured a large glass of Pinot Noir.

◆

I felt I'd hardly had time to turn around when Saturday was upon me and I had to transform myself into Jo for my meeting with Melissa. All this dressing up was beginning to get on my nerves, I suppose I'd sort of outgrown it, but where Melissa was concerned I'd no choice; all the more reason to speed things along. The idea of moving area to somewhere Liliad and I could be ourselves was becoming more attractive by the day.

I made sure I was at the café in good time and was gratified to find that Melissa was also a stickler for punctuality, arriving dead on noon.

'Hi, Jo, this is so kind of you but as I said there's really no need; I'm glad to help and anyway it's more *you* doing *me* a favour, taking the pressure off any concerns over cover while I'm away. I've been volunteering there for a few years now; I wouldn't like to leave them in a muddle.'

'I'm happy to help; they're a lovely crowd and it's always good to learn something new.' I handed Melissa the menu. 'Have a look and see what you'd like, I'll get us a couple of coffees.'

I had to admit the food was delicious; it was a pity I wouldn't be able to keep using the place. Between mouthfuls I said, 'You said you lived close to here?'

'Yeah, just over there in fact.' She pointed toward her apartment, its front windows visible behind the sparkling spray of the centre fountain.

'Really, you lucky thing; a lovely view and an excellent café on your doorstep; can't be bad!'

'Yes, I shall miss it.' Melissa looked slightly wistful as she gazed out the window.

'Oh, of course, your wedding; still, I expect you'll have a lovely new house to move into once you're married.'

'No, Andrew's insisting that we live in his apartment as it's so convenient for the hospital.' Realising that she might be sounding a bit disloyal she quickly added, 'It's a nice apartment, bigger than mine; it's just I don't like the area so much and it'll be a longer drive to work for me.'

'Where do you work?'

'At Walker Street Primary School. I love it but that's something else that will end shortly after my marriage.'

I raised my eyebrows questioningly. 'Why?'

'Andrew wants me to give it up; says he wants me to work for him. I've got a lot of admin experience and he says together we'll make a great team and my support will quicken his rise to the top of his profession.'

I gave her a sympathetic smile. 'If you don't mind my saying so, it all sounds a bit one-sided.'

She shrugged. 'I think so too but my parents are so keen on this marriage; they think Andrew's wonderful and a brilliant catch for their only child. Mum gave up her career to support Dad; they think it's what one should do. I can't get through to them that times have moved on.' Melissa sighed. 'Oh, listen to me! Andrew *is* wonderful *and* a brilliant catch; I guess I'm just scared of change. How about you? Are you in a relationship?'

I shook my head. 'No, not at all; don't get me wrong, I'm not a man-hater or anything; I've had relationships but they never seem to last. I think it's my fault really, don't want to give up my independence. I love my little flat; I call it my "bijou residence,"' I grinned widely, making an expansive gesture with my hand, 'and I enjoy my freedom but maybe, in truth, it's just because I haven't met the right guy.'

Melissa smiled encouragement, 'I'm sure you will one day. Don't listen to me and my doubts; it's most likely just pre-wedding nerves.'

'Yeah, I guess everyone has doubts. Wow, look at the time; I think I'd better make a move.'

Melissa picked up her bag at my cue and pushing back her chair said, 'Would you like to come to mine for a meal one evening, Jo. This has been great, it'd be nice to do it again and I can show you my apartment before it's sold.'

'I'd love that.'

'OK, although I should warn you I'm a hopeless cook; it'll probably end up being bought in.'

'No, don't do that. I *love* cooking; what if I bring the main course and you just worry about drinks, starters and desserts?'

Melissa looked thrilled, 'Are you sure you wouldn't mind? It seems a bit of a cheek.'

'Not at all; when should we say? I can do most evenings next week.'

'Let's say Thursday then; I shall look forward to it and maybe you can give me some cooking tips so Andrew doesn't have to starve once we're married!'

We parted at the door, Melissa back to her apartment and me into town to get some ideas for the meal.

CHAPTER 19

'Mrs Munroe!'

The last person I expected to see at my front door during a thunderstorm, Shirley Munroe looked like the proverbial 'drowned rat'; a very well fed rat it was true but sodden and bedraggled nonetheless. Had I have known it was her I wouldn't have answered but that's the problem with a flat in a converted house like mine, no intercom system simply separate doorbells.

'Annalee, I have to speak with you.' Water dripped off her wobbling chin resurrecting the disturbing memory of her husband, Inspector Munroe when he'd stood in my family's lounge at the start of his investigations into Addie Baxter's death. I recalled that on that occasion he too was soaking wet from a sudden downpour. As a child I'd counted, in fascinated silence, as rain droplets fell from the end of his nose; six as I recalled. I shook myself to dispel the image.

'Well in that case you'd better come in.'

Mrs Munroe followed me slowly up the stairs, her shoes squelching as she mounted each step.

'Would you mind coming into the kitchen; I'm just in the middle of preparing a casserole and I'd really like to get it finished.'

She didn't respond but simply followed me. 'Let me take your coat, you're wet through.'

With difficulty she wriggled out, having to peel the sleeves from her arms like a snake sloughing its skin. 'Please, take a seat.' I indicated one of the stools at the workbench. 'Can I get you a coffee or tea maybe?'

'No, thank you. I need to talk with you about Lily.'

I kept my head down concentrating on cutting up the carrots I'd just peeled.

'I was surprised not to have heard from you since Lily's death; I thought a phone call or card?'

Shit! Yes, that was a mistake. I should have thought; it would have been a more natural response. 'I'm sorry, I didn't mean anything by it, it's just I really didn't know what to say and I never do condolence cards, they always seem too impersonal, don't you think. It didn't mean I don't care.' I raised my head from chopping the carrots and looked across at her, tears trickling down my cheek.

Mrs Munroe's expression seemed cynical, her eyes narrowed as though she was focussing intently on my face. 'You cry very easily, don't you?' It sounded like an accusation.

'What? No, it's the onions I'd cut up just before you came; the scent is still on my fingers, I must have accidentally rubbed my eyes.'

'Oh, I expect that's it then.' She shifted slightly in her seat, her eyes still fixed on me; I felt I had to say something, her whole manner suggested doubt and suspicion.

'I really am dreadfully sorry about Lily. It's an awful tragedy. I was so shocked when I saw the news report.'

Mrs Munroe didn't respond directly but went off at a tangent. 'I've been thinking about the conversation we had in Sainsbury's café, you remember, you asked to meet me, said you wanted some ideas as to what to buy Lily for her birthday.'

I nodded then turned toward the sink to wash the braising beef to put in the casserole.

Mrs Munroe continued talking to my back. 'I told you that Lily was going to do the hike up Ben Carrick on her birthday; that was why she wasn't coming home.'

I continued washing the beef, ignoring her.

'Don't you recall?'

Turning toward her I placed the beef into the casserole dish before picking up a towel to dry my hands. Looking straight at her I said slowly and deliberately, carefully enunciating every word so there could be no mistake, 'No, Mrs Munroe I don't recall any such thing. You are mistaken. You told me Lily wouldn't be home for her birthday but you intimated it was because she was going to spend the time with her new found friends from the Art Centre. I was disappointed and, I admit, a little hurt. I'd told you she wasn't in touch with me so much anymore. I felt side-lined; I'd been looking forward to seeing her. I knew nothing about any walk up Ben Carrick; if I had I would have been very concerned.' As a parting shot I added, 'I'm surprised you weren't.'

Mrs Munroe stiffened at the implied criticism. 'I was concerned, of course I was but I knew Lily was a very sensible young woman and had been planning the hike for weeks. She was well prepared.'

'But not well enough, it seems.'

There was no answer to that. I picked up the bowl of dried woodland mushrooms I'd been soaking and walked across to the sink to drain them, Mrs Munroe watching me intently.

'What are those?'

Trying to get the conversation onto more mundane matters I gave a detailed reply. 'Dried mushrooms, they give the casserole a richer flavour than just the fresh ones. I put sun-dried tomatoes in as well, they give a very distinctive flavour. Do you do much cooking?'

'No, not really my thing and Eddie does such awkward hours, it's difficult.'

'How is Inspector Munroe? He must deal with tragedy so often in his job but I don't suppose it makes it any easier.'

'No, it doesn't.' Mrs Munroe shuffled down off the stool with some difficulty, her still damp skirt sticking to the seat. 'I need to go.'

'Of course,' I handed her her coat, 'If I can be of any help.'

She gave a barely perceptible nod of acknowledgement.

'You will let me know when the funeral is, won't you; I'd like to go?'

'I'm afraid the funeral is only going to be for closest family members, no-one else but you can make a donation to the mountain rescue service if you like; we feel that's best.'

'Of course, I understand; I'll be pleased to.'

I led the way down the stairs; as I opened the front door Mrs Munroe turned on the step. 'I know you had quite an influence on Lily, she spoke about you a lot; she thought you really cared about her, what with your intervention when she was shot; we both did.'

'Well, it's true, I did.'

Mrs Munroe didn't respond, merely looked hard into my eyes and then turned away, shuffling down the path.

Closing the door behind her I hurried back to the warmth of my kitchen and put the casserole for my evening with Melissa into the oven.

A donation to the mountain rescue service? Well, I suppose I'd have to; the bereaved get lists of those who donate so I'd better make sure I'm on it; keep up the appearance of concern if nothing else.

I wandered through into the lounge and sat with Liliad. 'That was awkward; I've a feeling Mrs Munroe is going to keep gnawing away but I'm sure there's nothing to link me to Lily's death; I was so careful.'

Liliad's expression didn't change.

◆

Things at work had slowed down a little so I was able to get home in good time on Thursday to don my other persona and leave the flat as Jo. Once the game was concluded I'd be glad to get rid of Jo. I didn't really like her very much; too much in the way of frills and feminine frippery. I was much more practical.

The casserole I'd made on the evening of Mrs Munroe's visit smelt divine. I placed it carefully in my cool bag and left, giving Liliad a brief goodbye kiss as I went. I still felt I couldn't use my car to go to Melissa's so had booked a taxi to pick me up at the corner of the street. I couldn't risk Carol downstairs paying too much attention to a waiting cab in case she saw a 'stranger' getting into it from my flat. As it was, I always had to sneak out the building. I had considered taking Jo's clothes and changing in a department store Ladies but then I'd have to carry everything with me which just might lead to awkward questions. No, on balance getting ready at home was the best; I just had to hope my luck held entering and leaving.

Arriving at Melissa's at seven I stood at the entrance door having pressed her buzzer, waiting for a reply when the door of the basement flat opened and the young chap I'd spoken to when delivering the flowers bounded up the steps almost colliding with me, such that he knocked into the cool bag threatening to spill the contents of the casserole.

Surprise and concern over the food made me exclaim, 'Careful!'

'Whoops, sorry; in a hurry.'

Just at that instant Melissa's voice came over the intercom. 'Hi, Jo come up; second floor, number ten.'

'Are you visiting Mel?' His smile was open and friendly. He glanced down at the cool bag, 'It's a bit cold and late for a picnic, isn't it?'

'We're not having a picnic; it's a casserole and you nearly made me spill it.'

'What can I say, sorry again; no harm done though,' he paused, studying my face intently. 'Have we met before? You seem vaguely familiar.'

'What? No, we haven't. Goodbye.' I pushed at the entrance door and made my escape as he called out, 'Enjoy your casserole; I shall be asking Mel tomorrow how good it was.' And with that the door slammed behind me.

Sod him! I'd met him so briefly when I'd delivered those flowers and I looked completely different then; dress, make up, no specs, the lot. How could he possibly think I was familiar? And if he thought that, had Dr Metcalfe suspected anything when we'd met at the theatre but he never intimated anything. I probably didn't have to worry but it was becoming clearer by the day that I needed to draw things to a conclusion sooner rather than later.

As I stepped out of the lift Melissa opened her front door. 'Jo, come in.'

The apartment was lovely, elegant yet unfussy. A suite of cream leather sofa and chairs were positioned looking out of the big picture window where garden lights illuminated the fountain; its spray dancing in the breeze, sparkling like myriad crystals. The kitchen/dining area wasn't a separate room as in my flat but was open plan at one end of the enormous lounge; Perfect for chatting with guests whilst putting the finishing touches to the meal.

Melissa hovered by the kitchen work surface, her hands fluttering over a starter of melon and parma ham, prettily fanned out on the plates. 'I hope this is OK as a starter; as I said, I'm not much good at this sort of thing.'

'It looks fine. Here,' I lifted the cool bag onto the surface and extracted the casserole, 'as it's still chilly outside I've made us a warming beef casserole with all the trimmings; we just need to pop it in the microwave for about ten minutes. There's a crunchy French stick as well so we can slice that up and some green beans to go with it – already prepared!'

'And I've got a bottle of red or white wine; which would you prefer?'

'Oh, the red please; perfect!'

Melissa, obviously slightly embarrassed about saying anything indicated my hands, covered in thin gauze gloves as I'd worn when applying the stage make-up.

'Are your hands OK, Jo? The make-up hasn't caused any issues has it?'

'No, it's not that; my own fault entirely. I used a soap in the ladies toilets in M&S and it obviously disagreed with me.' I carefully peeled back on the gloves exposing the raw, angry red skin on the back of my hand. 'It looks such a sight I'd rather keep them covered for now.' I silently congratulated myself on the effectiveness of the make-up; it didn't just apply to faces!

Melissa was all sympathy. 'It must be a constant nightmare.'

'It's not usually this bad; just having a rough patch. Still, never mind that; I'm hungry!'

An hour later, having finished the bottle of red we decided to open the white to accompany the dessert; a wonderful chocolate and ice cream concoction.

'I'm totally stuffed.' Melissa flopped onto the sofa, kicked off her shoes and tucked her legs up underneath her. I made my way across to an armchair, sinking gratefully into its cushions. 'I don't think I could eat another thing.'

Mel held out a box of dark chocolates. 'Well, maybe I could manage just one of those.' I leant forward and plucked my favourite out of its nest. 'Mm, these are nice; were they a gift?'

Melissa frowned slightly. 'I don't rightly know; in fact, I'm not even sure they were meant for me but in the absence of any information...'

'How come?'

'They were just there, outside my door when I got home from work one evening. No note on them; nothing to indicate who they were meant for or where they came from.'

I smiled, 'They must be from Dr Metcalfe, surely?'

'No, that's the thing; he says it's got nothing to do with him. The thing is, there were some flowers the week before but again, no note.'

'Oh, they *must* be from your fiancé; he's probably just playing silly games; either that or you've got a secret admirer. How lucky can one girl be?' I reached across and helped myself to another chocolate.

'That's the trouble I don't feel at all lucky. Andrew got quite nasty. It was ages before he'd believe me when I said I didn't know anything about it.'

'How strange; perhaps they weren't meant for you if there was nothing on them to indicate who they were intended for.'

Melissa poured herself some more wine. 'I know, that's what I said. I think he accepted it in the end but it was very uncomfortable for a while.'

Wriggling deeper into my seat cushions I suggested, 'Perhaps it was the guy in the basement flat; I met him on my way in.'

'What, Mark? I shouldn't think so; he's gay.'

I was genuinely surprised. 'Is he? He doesn't act like it; a bit macho I thought.'

'Just goes to show, you can't judge by appearances alone.'

'No, you can't, can you?' If only you knew, I thought. 'What does he do for a living?'

'He's at university, gave up his job and went back as a mature student. I think he's studying to be a forensic pathologist. I do know he's a stickler for detail, always practising his observational skills; he's pointed things out to me that I wouldn't have noticed in a million years.'

I felt the tension in my belly at the import of what Melissa was saying. I couldn't believe my bad luck; I'd need to keep my distance in future; I couldn't risk any more encounters with him just in case. I yawned and stretched. 'I booked my taxi for eleven so he'll be here shortly. I've had a lovely evening and I think your apartment is gorgeous. I'm quite envious.'

'Well it's up for sale.' Melissa wafted a hand to encompass the room.

'So it may be but it'll be way out of my price range. Thanks again for a lovely time.'

'My pleasure and thank you for the delicious casserole; let me have the recipe and maybe I can astound Andrew with my newly acquired culinary skills.'

'OK, will do.' Melissa's intercom rang. 'That'll be my taxi; bye Mel, see you again soon.'

'Bye, Jo; take care.'

I picked up my cool bag and hurried out. I had a lot of thinking to do, I hadn't yet decided on the method of elimination and time was getting short.

CHAPTER 20

Despite my earlier assurance to Liliad I found that Mrs Munroe's conviction that Lily's death was no accident played on my mind. I couldn't risk even the most tenuous of links and therefore decided to dispose of all my hiking gear; an expensive waste but one, in the interests of self-preservation, I was prepared to make.

I bundled up trousers, jacket, boots and backpack and hurried down to my car. To be doubly cautious I drove to the next town and donated the items to four separate charity shops. That should make them untraceable.

Arriving home I was just unlocking my front door when Carol came out of the downstairs flat. 'Hi, Annalee, are you OK?'

'Yes, fine thanks and you?'

'Yeah, I'm just off to the station; my sister's coming to stay for a few days so if you see a stranger letting themselves in and out of my flat, don't be alarmed. Talking of which, you've had a guest lately, haven't you?'

'Me? No.'

'That's strange, I was sure I'd seen someone going in and out of the building, Yes, I remember, we bumped into one another, quite literally, at the front door one evening; a young woman wearing specs. I remember I noticed them because they were quite large; a definite statement!' Carol gave a light chuckle but continued to look at me quizzically.

'Oh, no, she wasn't a guest; what I mean is, she wasn't staying overnight or anything; she's a work colleague just popped round a couple of times so we could sort out a work issue.'

'I see, OK. I didn't mean to pry but with just the two of us living here it seems sensible to keep an eye open for security reasons.'

'Absolutely; no problem. Bye.' I made my escape up the stairs cursing nosey neighbours.

Settling beside Liliad on the window seat I turned her head to look at me, holding her gently under the chin with one finger so that her head couldn't turn towards the window whilst I was talking. I needed her full attention. 'You know, Liliad I'm finding dealing with Melissa quite difficult; I just can't decide on the best way. There's been no time to form the kind of friendship that would lead to us going out or perhaps holidaying together when there might be more opportunity as she'd be away from her usual environment and associates. Neither can I cause her any kind of accident say at the theatre; far too many people about and time is running out. The wedding is in September, that's only four months away. I'd had years to plan Lily's demise; months to gain her confidence; it was simply bad luck I didn't succeed at the first attempt but with Melissa … I just don't know.'

Liliad seemed impassive to my monologue. I sighed, letting go my control of her head. To my surprise instead of turning to look out of the window her head turned slightly to the right and down. I followed her gaze. On the floor, tucked under an armchair, was a book of herbal remedies and medicinal plants. I recalled I'd borrowed it from the library some weeks before when I'd been feeling a bit under the weather. I'd never liked taking proprietary medicines and was investigating natural alternatives.

'Oh, my God, I'd forgotten I'd slid it under there.' I picked the book up and looked at the 'Return By' date. 'Damn! It's three weeks overdue; I'll have to pay a fine.' Idly flicking the pages an idea began to form. 'Liliad you are *so* clever. Why didn't I think of that? Now all I have to do is persuade Melissa that she'd just love us to have another meal together with me providing the main course again.'

I decided to lay low for a couple of weeks, doing nothing more than working and spending every evening in my flat while I carried out my research. I'd got a couple of useful books from the library, bought one that I'd seen by chance in a local bookstore and been on the internet. At the end of the fortnight I'd amassed a fair bit of knowledge;

now all I had to do was wait a short while so I didn't seem too pushy and then put the wheels in motion.

◆

A week later I was sitting in the canteen at work waiting for Robyn to join me when I overheard two women at another table.

'Oh my God, that's so gross! Here, Anne read this.' She handed the newspaper to her friend. Anne was silent for a few moments, reading.

'That's horrific; how awful and isn't that the detective who lost his daughter recently in that accident in Scotland. You wouldn't think he'd be up to investigating anything this soon would you, especially something as gruesome as that!'

'But how on earth could it have happened? I know those apartments; they have walled balconies, not the sort of thing you'd fall over accidentally. She must have climbed up.'

Anne folded up the newspaper and sighed. 'Probably drink or drug related. Maybe there was a party going on but it doesn't say. C'mon, lunch break's over, we'd better get back.'

They both pushed their chairs back and stood, leaving the newspaper on the table. Walking past me I heard Anne comment, 'What a ghastly way to go though,' she shuddered, 'doesn't bear thinking about.'

As soon as the door closed behind them I rose and collected their discarded paper, quickly opening it trying to find the article that had so appalled them both but before I located it, Robyn entered and beckoned me to join her. I folded the paper and reluctantly sat down beside her.

Despite surreptitiously trying to look at the newspaper at various intervals during the rest of the day it proved impossible and I had to wait until I was in my car leaving for home. I couldn't wait any longer, flinging my bag onto the passenger seat I settled myself behind the wheel and opened the paper.

It was the local edition, the front page taken up with details of the local election and a nasty pile-up on the dual carriageway into town. I found what I was looking for on the third page.

"DEATH PLUNGE OF WOMAN FROM APARTMENT BALCONY

A young woman has plunged to her death from the balcony of her second floor apartment at Cadogan Square, Endover in the early hours of Sunday morning. Melissa Hartnell, fiancée of the eminent psychiatrist, Dr Andrew Metcalfe and a teacher at Walker Street Primary School for the past four years was found at approximately two o'clock by the resident of the basement apartment, Mr Mark Jason.

Mr Jason, still visibly shaken several hours later said, "'I'm a bit of an insomniac and was just

*making a cup of tea when I heard this kind of
dull thud and a sort of … sort of squelch and
when I looked out I saw her impaled on my railings; I don't think I'll ever **stop** seeing her."*

*The investigating officer leading the enquiry is
DCI Eddie Munroe. Inspector Munroe, who lost
his daughter recently in equally tragic circumstances, has stated that, 'At present we are keeping
an open mind as to the circumstances that led to
this tragic incident. We will know more once the
post mortem has been carried out but until such
time as I have the pathologist's report and we've
completed our forensic examinations I'm not prepared to speculate on what may have occurred
here last night.'*

Dr Andrew Metcalfe was unavailable for comment."

I must have read the article at least three times before
I could compose myself enough to concentrate on the
drive home. Arriving back I rushed up the stairs to Liliad
clutching the newspaper to my chest, hardly able to control
my eagerness to let her know what had happened.

'Just listen to this, Liliad.' Reading the piece over again
the irony of the situation struck me. 'All that planning;
all that effort of changing my appearance and getting
involved with the amateur dramatic company and it was
all unnecessary; it's very inconsiderate of Melissa to do the
job for us!' I paused, turning everything over in my mind.

'Yet, you know, I can't understand how it could possibly be an accident. The balcony is bounded by a brick wall; it's only one brick thick but it came up to waist height; there's no way anyone could tumble over it accidentally even if they were drunk and Melissa didn't strike me as the sort of person who got drunk. It's very strange. Still, no matter; job done! May Dr Metcalfe have a long and miserable life ahead of him, we, on the other hand, can start planning our move away from here. Where would you like to live, Liliad?'

CHAPTER 21

We decided on Brighton; Liliad wanted to go back to where she'd come from and I loved being by the sea. Also, I felt I could get lost in Brighton's thriving gay community; not that I *was* gay, I wasn't but it would be a fun game to see how much I could convince people that I was.

I'd been in touch with my landlord and given him three months' notice of my intention to leave and given Robyn at work two. I was actually only obliged to give one month but I'd got on with Robyn so well and enjoyed my time at the Conference Centre I wanted to be as accommodating as I could.

'We'll be sorry to lose you, Annalee; me in particular. You've fitted in really well and your work has been a credit to you. Are you sure you won't change your mind?' Robyn asked hopefully.

'No, I'm afraid not. I've family up north that I haven't been close to for a while now and they're getting older and frailer. I feel I need to be nearer.'

'Of course, I understand; family must come first.'

I didn't want anyone knowing where I was actually going, preferring to cut all ties each time I moved on; much safer that way, hence the lie to Robyn.

For the first couple of weeks of my notice I spent most evenings with Liliad trawling the internet looking at flats for rent. They were quite expensive but I was still comfortable financially with the monies my parents had given me plus I'd been careful with my earnings and had amassed a fair bit in savings so I could afford something decent and in the more upmarket part of town. I confess that since being to Melissa's I'd yearned for something more modern and open plan and anyway, I figured I deserved it after all my hard work.

I'd always rented furnished apartments so only had personal belongings to transport which meant I could fit everything I wanted in my car so no need of removal companies being involved. Being as untraceable as possible was becoming a way of life.

I switched on the television just in time to get the end of the local news programme. Although initially not paying much attention I made my way towards the kitchen, thinking more of what to have for dinner than listening to the news when I heard the commentator mention Cadogan Square. I grabbed the remote and increased the sound.

'Investigations are still ongoing into the tragic death of Melissa Hartnell who fell from her second floor balcony on Sunday. Our Home Affairs correspondent, Matthew Meakin is outside the apartments in Cadogan Square. Matthew, what more can you tell us?'
'Thank you, Clive. Melissa Hartnell a teacher at Walker Street Primary School and fiancée of the eminent psychiatrist, Dr Andrew Metcalfe fell to her death in the early hours of Sunday morning from the balcony of her apartment here in Cadogan Square. Initially thought to be a tragic accident police are now considering the death as suspicious and would like to speak to anyone who may have information relevant to the case, however insignificant it might seem. Earlier today I spoke with DCI Eddie Munroe who is leading the investigation.'

The scene switched to outside Endover Police Headquarters. Inspector Munroe, gaunt as ever, stood before the camera; shoulders hunched, his head thrust forward on an overlong sinewy neck and his rapidly receding hairline giving the unfortunate impression of a vulture homing in on a cadaver.

'Inspector Munroe, is it correct that the police are no longer treating Miss Hartnell's death as an accident?'

Munroe's answer was as pedantic as ever.

'It would be correct to say that there are certain aspects of this case that cause us to question the likelihood of it being purely a tragic mishap.'
'Can you expand on that please?'

Munroe barely managed to stifle an exasperated sigh.

'The balconies at the Cadogan Square apartments are walled; narrow admittedly, only one width of bricks but they are a fair height, about waist level on someone of Miss Hartnell's stature; not a height one would expect anyone to accidentally tumble over. Also, it was a cold night with a fine drizzling rain; not the sort of night one would expect anyone to be out on their balcony especially in their nightclothes, without a dressing gown or shawl to protect them. However, until such time as we have the results of the post-mortem and toxicology report we are keeping an open mind as to what transpired. Thank you.'

Inspector Munroe, closing the interview emphatically, turned away from the camera and walked back into the police station, leaving the reporter with no choice but to hand back to the studio.

I dropped down onto my sofa, pondering what Inspector Munroe had said. I'd thought the same when I'd read the newspaper article; the balcony wall would surely have prevented any accidental fall and now, the knowledge that Melissa was only in her nightclothes lent more weight to it being suspicious. Surely something must have lured her out there on such a night, something that seemed urgent enough to not grab anything warmer to wear. It was all very curious but nothing to do with me. I had more interesting matters to attend to, my dinner for one.

◆

Strangely, I couldn't get out of my head what had happened to Melissa. Part of me felt slightly peeved that events had been taken out of my hands; how dare she spoil my game but also I was curious; I couldn't work out what could possibly have happened to cause her to fall plus I wanted to know how Dr Metcalfe was faring. I resolved to speak with Nurse Betty Fletcher.

I didn't want to go back into St Joseph's so asked Betty to meet me in town for a coffee. I made out I was considering a change of career into the caring profession and wanted her advice. She was only too pleased to assist.

'This is nice, Annalee.' Betty smiled warmly as I placed a latte on the table before her. 'You seem to have really found your feet lately and considering a change of career too; what's brought this on?'

I settled down opposite, leaning slightly forward over the table so I could speak quietly, confidentially. 'My time in St Joseph's made me take a long look at myself. I'd always been so self-focussed but your care of me and Dr Metcalfe's made me realise that there's a lot to be gained from helping others. Without the help you both gave me I wouldn't be where I am now; my own apartment, a decent job.' I paused, letting my words sink in. 'I want to do what you do; become a psychiatric nurse.'

Betty first looked pleased, flattered even but then doubtful. 'But if you have a good job now are you sure you want to give it up? It's a big step to go back to studying, financially especially.'

'I know but I've weighed it all up, I can afford it.' I reached across the table, lightly touching Betty's hand. 'I'm convinced it's what I want to do.'

Betty nodded, obviously pleased. 'Well, in that case, how can I help?'

We spent the next hour discussing various ways forward; possible courses and colleges, how to gain some practical experience in areas that would be beneficial to any applications I might make. I bought us another coffee each whilst Betty insisted on getting a couple of cream cakes to celebrate my new-found social conscience. Towards the end of our meeting I brought up Dr Metcalfe and Melissa.

'I was horrified to learn what had happened to Dr Metcalfe's fiancée; such a terrible tragedy. How's he coping?'

Betty's face crumpled slightly, a moistness springing to her eyes. 'I know; I can hardly believe it; they were both so happy, looking forward to the wedding in September.' She sniffed. 'She was such a beautiful young woman.'

'Yes she was; I remember seeing her photograph on Dr Metcalfe's desk. I expect he's taken some time off work, hasn't he?'

'No, we were all surprised but no, he hasn't. I guess he just wants to keep busy; we all have different ways of coping.'

'Do you think he'll stay in Endover? You'd think he'd want to get away from all the memories.'

'I've no idea what he'll do; he doesn't confide in me.'

I tried again. 'Has he ever said what he thinks might have happened? The television coverage says that the police think it's suspicious.'

Betty looked slightly perplexed, uncomfortable even. 'No, he hasn't. Why are you so interested, Annalee?'

'Just curious; I saw the photographs of the balconies; the walls seem too high for someone to just trip and fall over, don't you think?'

'I don't know what to think but I don't think it's my business to wonder, either. All this speculation simply hurts those that are left and that's not just Dr Metcalfe; there are her parents, the children she taught, her friends. It would be better if we all just remembered her for the lovely girl she was rather than indulging in gossip.'

How dare Betty take the high and mighty, holier than thou approach with me! I bit back the reply I'd like to make and instead lowered my head, as though shamed by her rebuke. 'Yes, you're quite right, Betty; I'm sorry, I didn't mean to be insensitive. I'd forgotten you'd actually met her; it's more personal for you.'

'Yes, I suppose it is.' Betty paused before continuing, 'I didn't mean to snap, Annalee it's just that everything is still so very raw. Well, I'd better be going. Good luck with everything and keep me posted.'

I watched as Betty made her way out of the café, cursing under my breath. I'd found out next to nothing although I couldn't help thinking it odd that Dr Metcalfe was continuing at work; that he hadn't taken any time off for grieving which I'd have thought was more natural. That, coupled with what I'd sensed when with Melissa, that things weren't quite as happily carefree and lovey-dovey as Betty seemed to think, made me even more curious but then I needed to remember that "curiosity killed the cat". You would have thought, after my time in St Joseph's that I'd have learnt that. I guess I'd been a bit incautious because I knew Melissa's death had nothing to do with me.

Nonetheless, I ought to have been more careful.

CHAPTER 22

I'd taken to buying the local newspaper because for some reason I couldn't get Melissa's demise out of my head and I wanted to know if the police investigations had moved on. For a couple of weeks there was nothing and then, relegated to page six, was a short column. Poor Melissa, so soon to become yesterday's news.

The article stated that the police, having spoken with Melissa's work colleagues and friends, had learnt that she had long been a volunteer at the Manor Lane Amateur Theatre. They'd therefore been questioning theatre members and were now trying to locate a Jo (Joanne) Simons, a recent volunteer who'd been assisting Melissa in the make-up department. If anyone knew Joanne's whereabouts please get in touch.

As I read I felt an unpleasant tingling at the back of my neck. I'd given a false address on my application form and had been careful not to disclose any personal information, false or otherwise. I'd also ensured I'd left no fingerprints backstage. I couldn't see any way the police could link me to Jo Simons; I'd even used a pay as you go phone with a different number to my usual mobile yet for some reason I felt slightly apprehensive.

I sat for a while analysing my fears. It was DCI Munroe heading the investigation that bothered me. He'd been suspicious of my friendship with his daughter from the very start and I suspected I was still very much in his thoughts. I knew he'd love to pin something on me and whatever else, I knew he wasn't stupid.

I closed my eyes and visualised each visit I'd made to the theatre as Jo Simons. I couldn't think of anything that would link me to her. There was that unfortunate encounter with Dr Metcalfe but I'd have thought if he was suspicious he would have acted on it by now. The only other thing I suddenly realised were the clothes in my wardrobe. I'd need to get rid of those just as I had the hiking gear I'd worn in Scotland.

I hurried through into the bedroom and tossed all of 'Jo's' clothes into a carrier bag along with her wig and designer specs. I wanted them out of the flat for although I couldn't think of any reason why the police should call I couldn't take the risk.

Grabbing my car keys I took the stairs two at a time, barrelling out of the front door just as Carol was on her way in, the carrier bag catching on her briefcase as we almost collided and ripping open, spilling some of its contents onto the front path.

Apologising for nearly knocking her over I grabbed at the items, stuffing them back into the bag as fast as I could as Carol bent to help me. Picking up the brown wig she held it aloft, 'Are you going to a fancy dress party?' she asked, a wide grin on her face.

'What? Oh no, not me; I hate anything like that. I've been getting some bits together for a friend who's making a dress up box for her daughter; I found that in a charity shop. Must dash 'cos I promised I'd take them round yesterday but I forgot. Bye.'

Stuffing the wig into the bag I gathered it into my arms and made for my car cursing my luck and drove off with no idea as to where on earth I was going.

Half an hour of aimless driving later I had an idea. I drove first to the local Sainsbury's and dumped half the items in their clothes recycling bin then continued on to the same facility at Morrisons to dispose of the rest. I then drove to our local park and making sure no-one was about, tossed the suspect phone into the middle of the wildlife lake before heading home.

Collapsing on the window seat beside Liliad I felt sure I'd covered all bases. There was now nothing to link me with Jo Simons and therefore Melissa.

◆

My two months' notice at the Conference Centre was over; Robyn presented me with a bottle of champagne to toast my new home together with a card of well wishes signed by all the team which I thought was nice considering I hadn't really been there that long. Consequently I was on something of a high the following week, luxuriating in not having to be up by a set time in the mornings. I lazed in bed until nine thirty, had leisurely breakfasts and slowly started going through my belongings discarding everything I didn't want to take with me to Brighton.

I was just getting ready to take some items to a local charity shop when my doorbell rang. Thinking it might be the landlord wanting to do a spot check before I left I hurried down the stairs.

'DC Wilson!'

'Detective *Sergeant* Wilson now, Miss Theakston. I'd like you to accompany me to the police station if you would.'

'Whatever for?'

'Detective Chief Inspector Munroe wishes to speak with you.'

'What about? Am I under arrest?'

'No, Miss Theakston you're not under arrest; Inspector Munroe feels you may be able to help us with our enquiries into the death of Melissa Hartnell. I expect you will have read about it in the papers.'

Wilson's tone had an arrogance that I'd normally associate with Munroe; obviously he was learning well under Munroe's tutelage.

'Of course I have, along with hundreds of others no doubt, but why should Inspector Munroe single me out to talk to.'

'You can ask him that at the station; please Miss Theakston, I need you to come with me now.'

I stared sullenly at Wilson, 'I expect I have little choice. Wait there, I need to get my coat and keys.' I made my way slowly up the stairs determined to be as aggravating as possible.

Sitting in the back of the police car on our way to the station I reflected on the history I had with DS Wilson in respect of the police raid shooting of Lily Munroe. He'd been a baby-faced naïve DC when I'd first encountered him; easy to manipulate. I smiled at the memory of the false leads and wild goose chases I'd sent him on but now that chubby, fresh-faced look had been replaced by a thinner, more care-worn expression although I sensed his loyalty to DCI Munroe was just as strong. I concluded that he wouldn't be so easy to 'play' as before; I needed to keep him at arms- length.

Entering the police station Wilson pointed me to a row of chairs opposite the main desk and told me to wait. I waited ten, fifteen, twenty minutes, deliberate I was sure, before Wilson reappeared and directed me to an interview room.

Sitting the far side of the table opposite the door, I closed my eyes and took a few deep breaths; I was *not* going to allow DCI Munroe to wind me up. Another ten minutes passed before the door opened and Inspector

Munroe entered the room. Barely glancing at me he settled himself on the chair opposite, thumbed through the folder he placed before him before closing it and looking directly at me.

'We meet again, Miss Theakston.'

I met his gaze. 'So it would seem, Inspector.' I kept my eyes locked on his; I was *not* going to be the one to look away first. Eventually Munroe broke the silence between us.

'As you know we're investigating the death of Melissa Hartnell, speaking with anyone who may have been associated with her, however tenuous the link.'

'So why are you talking to me? I didn't know her.'

'But you do know Dr Andrew Metcalfe, her fiancé from your stay at St Joseph's.'

'Well of course, I was under his care but I've never met her.'

'Perhaps not but you seem to have an avid interest in the couple.' Munroe paused, opening his folder once more and shuffling through the papers, selecting one sheet that he pretended to read. 'As part of our enquiries we've been speaking with staff at St Joseph's; a Nurse Betty Fletcher in particular. She tells us that on two separate occasions you've called on her and asked questions about both Dr Metcalfe and Miss Hartnell. Why would that be?'

I shrugged. 'Just casual chitchat really; having spent so many hours of therapy in Dr Metcalfe's room I'd obviously seen Melissa's photograph on his desk; a very pretty young woman as I recall. I suppose it felt a bit personal having had such close contact with Dr Metcalfe. I wondered how he was coping; I felt some concern, that's all.'

Munroe looked once more at the sheet of paper. 'Nurse Fletcher tells us that you specifically asked where Miss Hartnell worked.'

I feigned surprise. 'Did I? I don't recall.'

'Why would her place of work be of interest to you, Miss Theakston?'

I sighed and shrugged once more, fidgeting with the edge of the table as though bored. 'As I said, I don't recall; idle curiosity I expect.'

'Well, do you recall Nurse Fletcher's reply.'

I shook my head, 'No.'

'Let me remind you; it was Walker Street Primary School.'

'If you say so.'

'I do, Miss Theakston.' Munroe paused again and once more rifled through his papers before extracting another A4 sheet. 'A road traffic incident was reported to us a few weeks ago that took place outside Walker Street Primary School. A car almost hit a young boy and his mother as they were crossing the road. Do you recall *that*, Miss Theakston?'

I kept my face expressionless, 'No.'

'Well, you should; it was your car. The incident was reported by a Mrs Sandy Leatherhead; it was her child you almost hit.'

I shifted position on the hard seat, planting both feet firmly on the floor, grounding myself as I fought to control my racing mind. 'Yes, I do remember now. I don't know what Mrs Leatherhead reported but I did *not* nearly hit her son, I merely ran over his satchel that he'd slung into the road during a temper tantrum. Ask the school's lollipop lady; she saw the whole thing.'

Munroe leaned back on his chair, smugness evident on his face. 'We did and she supports what you say which was why we didn't pursue the matter at the time. However, my interest is in why you were at the school in the first place.'

I was beginning to get annoyed at Munroe's line of questioning which seemed deliberately obtuse. 'I wasn't *at* the school; I was driving past as countless other people must do.'

'It's a long way from your apartment; the other side of town in fact. What could you possibly want in that area?'

Angrily I pushed my chair back and stood, glowering down at DCI Munroe who remained seated. 'The supermarket; it's the only one in town.' I paused briefly. 'Inspector Munroe tell me, are you questioning everyone who has driven past Walker Street Primary School within the past few weeks? If so, I would imagine you have a very long task ahead of you.

I came here voluntarily to help with your enquiries although why you should think I could be of any help I have no idea; yet instead I'm subjected to puerile questions and veiled accusations with no substance in fact. I repeat, I have never met or spoken with Melissa Hartnell and I consider your attitude toward me to be little short of police harassment. Being charitable, I can only assume you are still suffering from your recent personal tragedy and that, coupled with your obvious animosity toward me you are determined to accuse me of any and every crime that comes across your desk!'

Resolutely I picked up my keys and coat and marched out of the room, stopping at the door I turned, 'If you continue to harass me I shall report you to the highest authority. Good day to you.'

Inspector Munroe made no attempt to stop me.

CHAPTER 23

I can't deny that the interview with Inspector Munroe had unsettled me. Sitting with Liliad on the window seat I sipped at the double brandy I'd poured, trying to calm the butterflies in my stomach.

'That man definitely has it in for me, Liliad and I have a horrible feeling he's never going to let go. The sooner we can lose ourselves in Brighton the better.'

There were only three weeks to wait; I'd booked us into a small hotel for a week when we first arrive to give us time to view apartments, we'd picked out six possibles on the internet but I wanted to see them for real before making a decision.

I took another sip of brandy, my mind returning inexorably to Melissa's death. The police were obviously convinced it was no accident yet there'd been no indication, from everything I'd read or heard, as to just what they did suspect; no post mortem results for instance. I couldn't help thinking that the police were keeping something back. Still, none of it was anything to do with me regardless of what DCI Munroe might like to think. I really must stop dwelling on it and get on with moving forward. Come to think of it, my car was due for its MOT and service so I'd better get that organised before the long journey down to Brighton; maybe I'd have it valeted as well; it would be nice to start our new life with everything spick and span.

A couple of days later I walked into town having just left my car at the garage when I bumped into Carol, my downstairs neighbour, coming out of the chemists.

'Hi, Annalee; I see you're leaving me.' Noticing my puzzled expression she continued by way of explanation, 'Your flat's up for let in the estate agents window.'

'Oh, I didn't think the landlord would have moved on it so soon; yes, I'm going back up north, family issues, you know how it is.'

'That's a shame, I shall miss you. I just hope the new tenant is as quiet as you've been.'

We'd subconsciously fallen into step and were passing the newsagents when Carol stopped and pointed at the shop window. 'Gosh, look at that; she looks so like your friend.'

In the window was an artist's impression of a young woman.

'POLICE NOTICE
The police are trying to trace the whereabouts of Joanne (Jo) Simons in connection with ongoing enquiries. If you recognise this person or have any information you believe may be of help please contact the police on the number below. All calls will be treated in the strictest confidence.'

The shock of seeing the poster stunned me for a moment so it was a few seconds before I could respond to Carol's comment. 'What friend?'

'I bumped into her or rather she bumped into me as she was leaving your flat a few weeks ago. She was in a dreadful hurry. Remember, I told you how I'd really noticed her large designer specs, they were such a feature! You told me she was a work colleague.'

'Oh yes, I'd forgotten.' I looked at the picture again. 'No, that's not Janet Streeter although I could see why you'd think it was; Janet does wear enormous specs.' I giggled, 'I always think she looks like an owl.'

Carol still looked doubtful but shrugged any uncertainty away. We'd just drawn level with the local bookstore so I made my escape, 'Ah, I need to pop in here; good to see you, Carol.'

'You too, drop your new address through my door before you leave; it'd be nice to keep in touch.'

Entering the bookshop I made my way upstairs where I knew they had a small coffee shop, bought a latte and settled down at a table to think. It was understandable that the police would be anxious to trace Jo Simons; someone who'd turned up at the theatre, worked with Melissa and then vanished; especially when they discovered that the address on her application form was bogus.

It had been pure bad luck Carol entering the house just as I was leaving a few weeks ago but hopefully I'd allayed her doubts on that score.

I decided I was worrying unnecessarily, best to put it out of my mind and continue preparations for Liliad and my move to Brighton. I finished my coffee and was making my way downstairs onto the High Street when I spotted Mrs Munroe on the pavement opposite. She was a sad figure, shoulders slumped, eyes focussed on the pavement yet I felt no sympathy. On her own admission it was her gossip that had focussed Inspector Munroe so persistently on my brother, Matt in respect of Addie Baxter's death. She didn't deserve to be happy; cause and effect, Mrs Munroe; it's a bitter lesson to learn, isn't it?

My mobile rang; it was the garage letting me know my car was ready. Perfect, I'd be home in time to catch the early evening news.

◆

I'd just cleared away the dinner things and settled myself on the sofa with a box of chocolates and a magazine when my doorbell rang. 'Oh, not again.'

I tossed the magazine onto the coffee table in exasperation and knelt next to Liliad to look out of the window. There didn't seem to be any car parked on the road outside so presumably it wasn't the police again and I couldn't see anyone on the garden path but if a visitor stood close up to the front door I couldn't see them anyway. I debated whether to just ignore it in the hope whoever it was would go away but there was another persistent ring, longer and more determined. I sighed and made my way down the stairs.

Mrs Munroe, wearing a mac that was so voluminous it looked more like a bell tent, was firmly planted on the doorstep, her whole demeanour one of resolute determination.

'Annalee, may I come in; I want to talk with you about Lily.'

I kept my hand firmly on the door not allowing it to open fully. 'I really don't think I want …'

'Please, Annalee Lily became very close to you what with the shooting and everything, I need to talk and you're the only one of her friends she kept in contact with.'

'Oh very well, you'd better come up.' I opened the door only a fraction more forcing Mrs Munroe to squeeze her massive frame through the narrow gap, the awkwardness of the movement caused her to catch her coat belt on the handle and spend an embarrassing few seconds trying to extricate herself.

I marched up the stairs leaving her struggling to keep up and flung myself down in an armchair, once again indicating the sofa opposite. I'd determined not to offer any refreshments; I wanted her gone as soon as possible.

Realising I wasn't going to offer any assistance she unbuttoned her coat and shrugged it off her shoulders as she sat perched uncomfortably on the edge of the sofa. Looking directly at me, the nervous hesitancy of her previous two visits seemed to have been replaced by a resolute firmness of purpose. 'As I said, I know Lily was very close to you, that she valued your opinion. I know she talked with you about going to Scotland, to the Art Centre. I want to know, how did she seem?'

'What do you mean … seem?'

'Was she nervous, anxious about going or excited, looking forward?'

'I got the impression she wanted to go; anyway, surely you must know how she felt, she said you were helping her so you must have talked about it a fair bit.'

'Yes we did but it was in a very matter of fact way, the formalities and practicalities and so forth; Lily didn't talk about her feelings very much.' The admission obviously caused her pain.

Thinking back to my conversation with Lily in the café I realised I could cause another upset in the Munroe household – this got better and better! 'I don't mean to speak out of turn but …'

Mrs Munroe leant slightly forward, eager for anything it seemed. 'Yes…?'

'Well, she did tell me that she was sick of her father's interference in her life; that he was always checking up on her, 'suffocating' was the word I think she used. I may be wrong but I got the impression that she was using the course as an excuse to get away.'

Mrs Munroe visibly stiffened; her face muscles rigid as she compressed her lips into a tight line. She was silent for a few moments until, with obvious difficulty asked, 'Did Lily ever give you the impression she might harm herself?'

I pondered her question pretending serious consideration. If I could encourage that view of Lily's mental state it could only lessen suspicion of foul play and perhaps put a halt to Mrs Munroe's digging. 'Mrs Munroe, I'm no expert in those things; I'd really rather not say.'

'Please, Annalee it's important.'

Feigning awkward hesitancy I replied, 'Well, she always seemed to be putting a brave face on things but deep down I think she was still badly shook up from the shooting. I mean, in the café, we were having coffee and a car outside backfired and she nearly jumped off her seat, spilt her coffee everywhere. It was as though the slightest thing could upset her; her nerves were so on the edge and then, of course, she was very upset that Barry had ended their relationship – I think she blamed her father for that.' I paused to let my words sink in. 'Why do you ask? Is it thought she committed suicide?'

A small tear ran down Mrs Munroe's cheek unheeded. 'That's what her father thinks.'

'And … do you?'

Mrs Munroe sighed, closed her eyes as if exhausted and slowly shook her head. 'No, I believe she was stronger than that; something happened up there on that mountain, I'm sure of it.'

'But you said she'd planned all along to do the hike alone, maybe it was a deliberate decision; that she knew what she was going to do, that's why she didn't want anyone with her. It seems the most likely.'

Mrs Munroe considered for a moment. 'No, I won't tarnish her memory by believing that.' Gathering her coat up onto her shoulders, she heaved herself up off my low sofa. Turning toward the window she spotted Liliad. 'I see you still have the marionette.'

I followed her gaze and smiled, 'Yes, I do.'

'Lily said you were very fond of her; that she was special to you. It's a strange name, Liliad; I've never heard of it before.'

'No, I made it up.'

She turned to face me, 'I'll say goodbye then, Annalee; thank you for talking to me; I won't bother you again.'

I followed her out onto my landing and down the stairs, noting that despite her bulk Mrs Munroe sagged as if all the fight had gone out of her. In the lobby she turned and as if it was an afterthought said, 'They found her camera, you know but I haven't been able to look at the photos she took; maybe in time it won't be so painful.'

I felt my breath catch in my throat. 'But will there be any photos? I mean surely it was damaged in the fall or by the weather.'

'No, remarkable isn't it. The strap was still around her neck and it seems she must have clutched it to her as she fell. When they found her she was laying on top of it so protecting it from the elements. It's only a little digital camera but they reckon the photos will still be OK. We only received it yesterday and I haven't told Eddie yet; I don't want him taking it from me or making me look at things before I'm ready. Apparently the mountain rescue team had put it to one side in their vehicle and it got covered up with other things, they've only recently found it. They were very apologetic but it's just one of those things; I'm not going to complain. They found her; that's all that really counts.'

'Of course, I understand. Goodbye Mrs Munroe.'

As I closed the door behind her my mind relived that final climb up Ben Carrick.

CHAPTER 24

I spent a restless night, my sleep filled with dreams of Ben Carrick. At some points on the trail Lily was behind me taking photographs I was unaware of; she waved to some people on the trail ahead of us; she'd left a message at the Art Centre advising that I might visit. I tossed and turned my way through the night, waking with a start whilst it was still dark, covered in clammy perspiration. For the first few seconds of consciousness I thought it was all real, fear of discovery creeping over me with the relentless persistence of a rising tide; suffocating the breath from me.

I dragged myself out of bed; padding to the bathroom I splashed cold water on my face, then to the kitchen to make a strong cup of coffee. Settling on the sofa I looked across at Liliad still snuggled down beneath her blanket, eyes tightly shut. It was obvious I wasn't going to get any help from that quarter. I needed to think things through; be logical. I closed my eyes and once more played out the whole day in my mind; driving to the car park, hiding until Lily arrived, keeping a fair distance behind her as she began her hike. I focussed my memory on every step; I was sure that at no point did she turn around and see me much less take a photograph. She couldn't have done or her shock wouldn't have been so obvious when I made contact.

We'd walked together the rest of the way; I couldn't have missed her taking my photograph and on the summit plateau I didn't take my eyes off her, not for a second. No, wait a minute; I did just briefly when I checked to ensure no other walkers were in sight. I screwed my eyes tighter, trying to relive that moment in time; the camera was around her neck, she had her fingers on it but it was nowhere near her eyes, it was down by her chest. I relaxed, nothing to worry about I was sure.

The release of tension made me feel quite light-headed. I made my way back to the kitchen to prepare some breakfast and another coffee before I resumed our packing.

◆

By three thirty in the afternoon I figured I'd done as much packing as I usefully could. Feeling a bit edgy I began to wish I hadn't given the landlord such a long notice. I supposed we could just leave, go down to Brighton earlier than intended. There was nothing to stay for any more, perhaps that's what we'd do.

I entered the lounge and sat by Liliad on the window seat. She was gazing out towards St Joseph's yet again; I felt slightly annoyed and exasperated by her fixation, maybe leaving sooner would be the best idea.

I was reaching for my mobile, thinking I'd telephone the hotel I'd booked into and see if we could check in a week earlier when I was distracted by footsteps outside. Kneeling on the window seat to look I was surprised to see DCI Munroe walking up the path with DS Wilson in tow. 'Oh no, what the hell is it this time?' As far as I was concerned my 'game' with DCI Munroe had ended with the death of Lily although watching his suffering was always a pleasure but it seems he's determined to keep it going; if so I was willing to play along.

The doorbell rang. I took my time going down the stairs affecting a flowing elegance that helped calm and control my mind. By the time I opened the front door I was ready for him. 'DCI Munroe,' I looked past him, 'oh and DS Wilson, how nice; how may I help you both?' I smiled sweetly.

'Miss Theakston, may we come in; I've a few more questions.' Inspector Munroe's look was one of serious formality.

'I can't imagine what about, Inspector but,' I stood back from the door and waved my arm inwards, 'by all means, be my guest.'

The two entered, pausing in the lobby like perfect gentlemen to let me mount the stairs first. Entering my lounge I indicated the sofa which Wilson alone accepted, Munroe preferring to stand.

'May I offer you a coffee or tea, perhaps?'

'This isn't a social call, Miss Theakston.' Munroe adopted a 'let's get down to business' tone.

'Of course, Inspector I was merely being civil but no matter. However, *I would* like a coffee so if you'll excuse me.' Before he could object I turned and walked into the kitchen.

Ten minutes later I returned to the lounge to find Wilson where I'd left him, perched on the edge of my sofa and Munroe by Liliad, gazing out of the window, his hands in his jacket pockets and back ramrod straight, as though holding his temper in check.

I positioned myself in the armchair and smiled across at Wilson, 'Are you sure I can't tempt you, Sergeant; it'll only take a moment.'

Wilson momentarily looked keen but at a glare from Munroe declined with a disappointed shake of his head. Turning, Munroe looked directly at me. 'Miss Theakston, if you're sure you're ready…'

'Oh, absolutely, Inspector; you have my full attention.'

Munroe couldn't hide his annoyance. 'Miss Theakston, as you know, we're investigating the death of Melissa Hartnell …'

'*Still*, Inspector?'

'Yes, Miss Theakston, still. We had a phone call late yesterday from your neighbour stating that she thought she might have recognised our artist's impression of Joanne Simons.'

'Who?'

'Miss Theakston, let's not play games.'

'Is that what we're doing, Inspector; I wasn't aware.'

Munroe's tone was almost a snarl. 'I do not believe you are entirely unaware of the name; it's been in the papers and in shop windows and your neighbour advises that she brought one such notice to your attention only yesterday.'

'Oh yes, I do remember now.' I deliberately looked past Munroe to DS Wilson and addressed myself to him. 'Yes, Carol thought she looked very much like a friend of mine but she was mistaken.'

'May I have the friend's name?' Munroe shifted position, blocking my view of Wilson; his tall frame towering above and leaning slightly toward me like the extended jib of a crane. I returned his stare.

'Janet Streeter.'

'Address?'

'I'm afraid I don't have one.'

Munroe clenched his hands; I was really getting under his skin. 'We understand that you told your neighbour that this Janet was a work colleague but we've been in touch with the Conference Centre, a Miss Robyn Campbell, who says they have no-one of that name on their staff.'

This was becoming a game of verbal ping pong; most enjoyable. 'I expect she would say that, it's true.'

'Then …?'

'Carol, my neighbour as you keep referring to her, must have misunderstood me; Janet is not a current work colleague but one from a previous employment. I hadn't seen her in years but she was this way apparently visiting an aunt and we bumped into one another in town; a happy coincidence. I invited her back to catch up on old times.'

'Your neighbour says you said you were going over some work issues.'

'Then she is mistaken again, Inspector; I'm sure I never said any such thing.'

Munroe turned away from me, frustration evident in his manner and signalling to DS Wilson, walked back towards the window leaving Wilson to say, 'Miss Theakston, with your permission we'd like to conduct a search of these premises.'

I couldn't keep the surprise out of my voice, 'Whatever for? On what grounds?'

Munroe turned from his perusal of the street. 'You may remember when I was investigating the apparent murder of your student, Barry Mason's father. At that time we had reports of a young woman calling on Barry's landlord and his foster parents; a young woman who, although not fully answering your description, was of a similar build and height. Given those similarities and your apparent avid interest in the case, we had good reason to suspect the young woman was yourself.'

'But it wasn't, was it, Inspector?'

'It's correct that we couldn't *prove* otherwise; however, speaking with your parents when you were in the hospital we learnt that you had, as a child, spent an inordinate amount of time dressing up, pretending to be someone else. Your parents tell us you became quite accomplished at it, practised to the point of obsession. Hence it is not beyond a reasonable assumption that you have retained those skills. The description we've been given of Joanne Simons as to height, weight and general demeanour leave us with similar suspicions.'

I passed a look of complete incredulity towards Wilson who shuffled uncomfortably on the sofa. 'I don't believe I'm hearing this; what a ridiculous line of enquiry. A young girl likes playing dress up and you carry that into her adulthood and accuse her of being some sort of con artist. It beggars belief! Plus there must be hundreds, thousands of women of my approximate build and height yet you focus on me.'

Munroe raised his voice; I could tell his patience was wearing thin. 'In addition to what I've just said, your neighbour says she bumped into you as you were leaving the flat one day and you dropped a bag containing a brown wig.'

I deliberately raised my voice in response. 'And I explained that to Carol at the time which I assume she's had the grace to apprise you of.' I gave an exasperated sigh and looked again at Wilson. 'Do you have a warrant?'

Wilson reddened slightly, standing up to give more authority to his reply. 'Not at present but we can apply and come back later.'

'Well, in my humble opinion you don't have anything like enough grounds to obtain a warrant but, simply because I have absolutely nothing to hide and so that I cannot be accused of being deliberately obstructive and,' I rose from my seat, 'because I'm always happy to help the police with their enquiries, search away DS Wilson. I'm going to get another cup of coffee.'

I strode through into the kitchen and busied myself with getting my drink. Talk about blabbermouth neighbours; I'd make damn sure when Liliad and I were in Brighton I don't make friends with anyone.

I could hear Wilson rummaging around in my wardrobe and chest of drawers and glared at Munroe. 'He'd better be putting everything back where he finds it.'

'He will, Miss Theakston. While we're waiting, I understand from your boss at the Conference Centre that you've left recently, going up north for family issues I believe she said.'

I sipped at my coffee, making no reply.

'Is that correct?'

'I don't consider it's any of your business one way or the other, Inspector.'

'Perhaps not just at this moment but whilst I consider you are still of interest in respect of my current enquiries

I would advise you not to leave the area without letting me know.'

At that moment DS Wilson returned to the lounge giving a brief shake of his head to Munroe, who pursed his lips in a tight line of barely suppressed anger. Turning his back on the room once more Munroe moved towards Liliad, sitting quietly on the window seat. 'I see you still have the doll.'

'*Don't touch her*' I exclaimed as he stretched out his hand toward her. He stopped mid-movement. 'A little strange isn't it, a woman of your age wanting a doll.'

'She isn't a doll, she's a marionette; it's quite different.'

'If you say so, Miss Theakston, if you say so.'

'Is that all, Inspector or am I now to be arrested for owning a marionette.'

Munroe turned and beckoned to Wilson. 'No, that's all … for now. We'll see ourselves out.'

I stayed where I was listening to their footsteps down the stairs and the bang of the front door. Game to me, I think.

CHAPTER 25

Munroe and Wilson's visit had clinched it – Liliad and I were leaving – now. I'd rung the hotel and managed to bring my booking forward a week and then drove to the garage to fill the car with petrol ready for the long journey. Back at the flat I laid out the clothes I'd wear for travelling and packed just about everything else. Another day and we'd leave Endover for good.

I couldn't say I was sorry to go; I'd never been one for putting down roots, always getting a thrill out of starting afresh, creating a new life and persona. Also, I was feeling a little jaded and Liliad's persistent focus on St Joseph's was really beginning to grate. We *both* needed to leave. As for informing Inspector Munroe of my intentions – no chance and if he made enquiries as to my whereabouts both Robyn and Carol would say the same, that I'd moved up north. I couldn't see that he'd know where to start.

I couldn't check into the hotel until after two so there was no point leaving very early and, in any case, I wanted to miss the rush hour traffic. The weather wasn't brilliant either, a fine drizzle that threatened to mutate into heavier rain meant I didn't want to be killing time in Brighton until I could check in. Consequently I got up late and was just settling down to a cooked breakfast when my doorbell rang. 'Oh, for crying out loud; what is it now? This place is getting like Piccadilly Circus!'

I took the stairs two at a time, determined to give whoever it was the minimum of time and return to my breakfast before it was ruined. Flinging open the door the grey light of a miserable morning was completely blocked out by a wall of dark uniforms. Two burly policemen stood shoulder to shoulder, their size twelve boots planted firmly on the doorstep. I was so surprised I merely gaped at them as they briefly parted to allow DS Wilson to the fore. Waving a piece of paper in my face he crowed, 'Miss Theakston, I have a warrant here to search your premises; please stand aside.'

Wilson strode forward, the two uniformed officers close behind leaving me pressed back against the wall as they hurried up the stairs. I stood where I was for a few seconds, completely stunned and then ran up the stairs to find all three in my bedroom, opening the wardrobe and pulling open drawers.

'Sergeant, what's the meaning of this?'

Wilson didn't answer but said, 'These cupboards and drawers are surprisingly bare. Where are your clothes,

Miss Theakston?' He glanced round the room and spotted my suitcase and a few boxes stacked in a corner. 'Are you going somewhere?'

I ignored the question and instead went on the attack. 'You searched my flat only yesterday and didn't find anything. What is it you're looking for?'

Wilson looked at me with thinly veiled hatred. 'This is a separate matter and when we've concluded our search I shall require you to accompany me to the police station.'

'*Why?* What's this all about?'

Having finished ransacking my bedroom, including opening my suitcase and packing boxes all three moved out onto the landing where there were a couple of built in storage cupboards and continued their search. Obviously drawing a blank they then entered the lounge. The window seat on which Liliad sat was also a storage unit. Before I could stop him Wilson walked over and unceremoniously hoiked Liliad off her seat, almost tossing her onto my sofa. I raced across and gathered her into my arms. 'How *dare* you?' I glared at Wilson who merely shrugged as he lifted the seat lid and rifled through its contents. 'None of that stuff is mine, it belongs to the landlord,' I explained as he sorted through spare curtains, cushions, a pot of paint and some wall filler.

By now one of the uniformed officers had worked through into my kitchen where I could hear him opening and closing cupboards and slamming drawers shut. I tried again to get some explanation. 'Sergeant Wilson, just what on earth are you looking for? If you tell me what it is I might be able to save us all a lot of wasted time.'

Again Wilson ignored me, instead acknowledging the shake of head from both officers. 'OK, Miss Theakston, come with me please.'

The two officers closed in on either side of me as I realised I was still clutching Liliad to my chest. Looking at all three it was obvious that Wilson wasn't going to take 'No' for an answer. I placed Liliad back on the window seat, carefully tucking her strings behind the cushion. Taking hold of my handbag I took a deep breath and allowed myself to be escorted down the stairs.

Sat in the back of the car next to one of the uniformed officers with the other driving and Wilson in the front passenger seat it was obvious from the outset that I wasn't going to be enlightened as to anything on our way to the police station, all three staring pointedly out of the windows and ignoring me.

At the station I was ushered immediately into an interview room on the first floor, a WPC being stationed just inside the door; I was damn sure she wasn't there to keep me company. For once I wasn't kept waiting long as five minutes later DS Wilson entered the room.

'No Detective Chief Inspector Munroe today, Sergeant? I feel quite bereft.'

Wilson ignored my sarcasm and went to switch on the tape recorder. 'Am I under arrest?'

'No, Miss Theakston, we merely wish to ask you a few questions to assist with our enquiries.'

'Then I don't see the need to record this interview, Sergeant. If you persist I shall say nothing until I have a solicitor present.'

Obviously annoyed Wilson agreed and launched straight in with his first question. 'Do you own or have you ever owned a green wax jacket?'

I was completely taken aback. 'I beg your pardon? What are you now – the fashion police?'

'Please, Miss Theakston, just answer the question.'

'Is that what you were looking for in my flat? Well, I'm sorry to disappoint you but no, I don't and never have owned a green wax jacket but if you're so desperate I'm sure I can tell you where you can buy one.'

Wilson didn't respond but opened the file he'd brought with him. Before he could say anything further I asked, 'Where is Inspector Munroe today? I'm surprised something as important as an article of my clothing isn't receiving his personal attention.'

Wilson darted a look of intense dislike in my direction. 'DCI Munroe is occupied on another matter.'

'Oh, investigating the tragic death of Melissa Hartnell, I suppose. How's that progressing? It seems to have been going on for an awfully long time.'

Ignoring my question yet again Wilson pulled a photograph from the folder and sat studying it for some time without letting me see it. Then, placing it back in the folder he sat back in his chair. 'Miss Theakston, I understand from colleagues at your place of work that you had a holiday recently. Is that correct?'

There was no point denying it, it would be in Robyn's records. 'Yes, that's correct.'

'Your boss, Ms Robyn Campbell, says you told her it was a family gathering. Which family members did it include?'

'I don't see why …?'

'As I understand it you have no family in this country; indeed, speaking with your parents who immigrated to Australia …'

So *that's* where they went, I couldn't say I was surprised.

'…there *is* no family; no relatives in this country or indeed any other, only themselves with whom you no longer have contact. So, where did you go for those two weeks?'

'Perhaps I didn't go anywhere, just took the time off work and stayed at home.'

'Then why tell Ms Campbell such a cock and bull story about how important it was that you attended a family party?'

I shrugged and hung my head slightly as if I found my admission uncomfortable. 'I was embarrassed to admit I had nowhere to go or anyone to share my holiday with. It's difficult being a single woman.'

Wilson looked at me with disbelief. He leant forward, resting his forearms on the table between us. 'But why were *those* two weeks so important? If you were just staying at home it could be anytime, surely? Ms Campbell said your insistence made things quite awkward work-wise.'

I didn't answer for a moment, merely stared blank-faced at Wilson, leaning back in my chair as I did so, adopting an air of insouciance. Avoiding answering his question I asked one of my own. 'Sergeant, would you please be good enough to inform me why you are interrogating me and over such inconsequential matters as my wardrobe and how I spend my annual leave.'

Instead of answering Wilson re-opened his folder and extracted a sheet of paper which he perused before addressing me once more. 'If you stayed at home for those two weeks can you explain why we have CCTV footage of you boarding the Edinburgh Express at Kings Cross on the morning of 25 May, the start of your annual leave.'

Although Wilson's assertion was a shock I managed to retain an air of bemused indifference. 'You can't have; I didn't.'

'But we do, Miss Theakston.' He handed across the print out of the CCTV footage.

'Well, I do have to concede that she does look remarkably like me but it most certainly isn't. They say everyone has a doppelganger, someone who looks exactly like them. Perhaps that's who it is. Do you have any other evidence to support your accusation?'

Obviously hoping to disarm me Wilson said, 'We are currently obtaining a warrant to access your bank account; no doubt that will reveal relevant transactions.'

I shifted in my chair and nonchalantly tucked a stray hair behind my ear. 'By all means, please access my bank account; you won't find anything incriminating. What you will find is that I've always bought my train fares, into London and so forth, by card so it's quite inconceivable that I should not do so on such an expensive journey, don't you think?'

Wilson said nothing but remained stony-faced. Opening the folder once more, he removed the photograph for a second time and sat studying it for a few minutes before sliding it toward me across the table.

I affected an air of total indifference as I glanced at it. 'What am I meant to be looking at? If this has been taken by a police photographer he really needs more training; it's very poor.'

'That is the last photograph taken by Lily Munroe.' Wilson stared intently at me, obviously hoping for some reaction. I could feel a very slight trickle of sweat run down my back but maintained my composure.

'Really; then I hope the rest are better than this effort, it's dreadful.'

I could feel the tension in the room mounting as Wilson struggled to keep his temper. Prodding at the photograph he said, 'Look carefully, Miss Theakston, what can you see?'

I pretended to examine it closely, 'Well, there's a lot of grey sky but as I said, it's very blurry.'

'Look at the right hand side, what do you see there?'

I peered closer, 'I'm not sure. Sorry, I can't help you.'

'We don't need your help, Miss Theakston; we know what it is; it's the arm and shoulder of a person.'

I leant over the photo again. 'Oh, so it is, I can see that now; how very clever of you.'

Wilson continued as if I hadn't spoken. 'A person wearing a green wax jacket.'

'If you say so, Sergeant I'll take your word for it but what's this got to do with me?' I paused for the briefest second. 'Oh, now I understand why you wanted to know if *I* had a jacket like that ...' I looked straight into Wilson's eyes, '... but I don't, do I? Let me see if I'm reading this correctly. I happen to take two weeks annual leave during which time, by sheer coincidence, Inspector Munroe's daughter dies and you therefore conclude that I must somehow be involved in her death. Tell me, Sergeant, are you interviewing anyone else in this regard?'

Wilson looked sheepish, refusing to answer.

'Quite. I would think, on the spurious circumstantial evidence you've presented so far, that I have good reason to suspect the police of harassment. However, I'm always happy to help, especially as Lily was a friend of mine.'

Wilson glared back but said nothing; I waited a minute and then took the initiative. 'Well, Sergeant if I'm not under arrest I consider this interview at an end. I'm sorry I can't be of more help but now I understand why DCI Munroe wasn't present – conflict of interest I believe you call it. However, please tell Inspector Munroe that

I'm truly sorry for his loss and it does appear that Mrs Munroe is right.'

Wilson looked momentarily puzzled.

'Her TV appearance; she maintained that Lily's fall wasn't an accident or a suicide despite Inspector Munroe believing it was. Perhaps the police should enrol Mrs Munroe, she seems far more perceptive than her husband!'

I grinned broadly as I picked up my handbag and stood. 'I'll see myself out.'

'No, the WPC will walk you to the door.'

'As you wish.'

'And Miss Theakston, you are still a person of interest so I would advise you, packing or not, not to leave the area any time soon,.'

I merely nodded and followed the WPC without a backward glance at Wilson. What an amateur; no wonder the police clear-up rate is so low.

I walked home which gave me time to think. So, Mrs Munroe had obviously plucked up the courage to look at the photos on Lily's camera and what she saw confirmed her suspicions; there was someone up on Ben Carrick with Lily and Mrs Munroe or at least Inspector Munroe, suspected it was me. Slightly worrying but everything they had was circumstantial and I was convinced I'd covered my tracks in Scotland sufficiently well.

Lily must have taken the photograph as she went over the edge but not as a deliberate act. I recalled she was just turning toward me as I collided with her; her hands were still on the camera; she must have clicked by reflex, that's why most of the photo was nothing but sky. Thank goodness the angle was such that it only caught my left shoulder and arm; it could be anyone. Still, it was a close thing.

CHAPTER 26

When I got home I repacked everything in the boxes and suitcase for despite DS Wilson's assurance his officers had left things in a jumbled heap. I was a bit concerned at the CCTV coverage from Kings Cross Station and wondered if they had also been looking for the clothes I was wearing at that time but the image was quite grainy and denim jeans and T-shirt is hardly distinctive attire. It would be next to impossible to prove they were mine.

It took three trips up and down the stairs and out into the back of the property to pack my car but finally it was done. Returning to the lounge I picked Liliad up and held her close as we both gazed for the last time at the roof top of St Joseph's. 'You see, I told you not to worry and I always keep my promises.'

Liliad's head turned toward me and gently rested on my shoulder; I could have sworn I heard her sigh. I took a final look around the flat making sure I hadn't missed anything. Leaving the keys on the coffee table I walked down the stairs, firmly closing the bottom door behind me, knowing it would lock automatically on the Yale. 'Decision made,' I murmured as I stepped out of the front door and headed toward my car. Strapping Liliad into the front passenger seat I settled myself behind the wheel, took a deep breath and pulled out of the car park.

Mid-afternoon the traffic in town was relatively light so we made good progress onto the ring road. We were about three sets of traffic lights from the turning I would have to make when I caught sight of a police car in my rear view mirror. I didn't pay it much heed, they were always patrolling the ring road as certain sections were notorious for 'boy racers' and they didn't seem to be in much of a hurry; just keeping their place in the line of cars behind me.

By the time I'd reached the third set of traffic lights and was indicating to make my turning the police car was directly behind me, the intervening vehicles having turned off at various stages. I still wasn't concerned despite knowing that I'd been instructed on more than one occasion not to leave the area without notifying the police first but as I made my turn they followed me. They didn't seem to be making any attempt to stop me but just to be on the safe side I decided to pull into a large shopping complex on the outskirts of town.

Knowing there was another exit from the complex I cruised around until I found a space near it behind one of the buildings. I parked and walked into the Mall, bought a coffee and waited for about half an hour. It didn't appear that the police car had followed me but just in case they were waiting at the entrance I decided to leave by the alternative exit. It would mean a tortuous drive to get back to my chosen route but I figured it was worth the inconvenience.

Back in my car I eased my way out back into the traffic; good, no police vehicle in sight. Once back onto the correct road towards Brighton I relaxed, turning on the radio to my favourite local music channel just at the point when they were giving the hourly news bulletin.

> *"An investigation has recently been opened into the death of Lily Munroe, daughter of DCI Eddie Munroe. Originally thought to be suicide or a tragic accident new evidence has emerged suggesting Miss Munroe may have been the victim of an assault. Police are now concentrating their enquiries in Scotland.*
> *The investigation into the death of Melissa Hartnell is still ongoing, the police recently revealing that the post mortem examination has confirmed that Miss Hartnell was murdered but for the present they are not disclosing any more details."*

I grinned at Liliad sitting mute beside me. 'Good luck to them; they won't find anything up in Scotland, I was *so* careful and anyway, they won't find us, will they?' Pausing at a T- junction I chewed at my bottom lip, considering Melissa's case. 'Strange that the police still aren't disclosing exactly what happened to Melissa; perhaps they think she was thrown over the balcony but there's been no reports of any altercation or argument. You'd have thought the neighbours would have said something if there was; I can't think what could have caused her to fall. Still, no matter, for once it really has got nothing to do with us!' I chuckled lightly at the irony and pulled out into a gap in the traffic.

The journey was going well; we were coasting along nicely with only a few miles more to the motorway when I noticed a patrol car parked in a layby on the dual carriage-way. It pulled out just as I passed, falling in behind me. I checked my speed; no problem there. I glanced at Liliad who was staring fixedly ahead. The police suddenly pulled alongside me, blue light flashing. I looked anxiously across as the officer in the passenger seat gesticulated that they wanted me to pull over into the next layby. There was no point putting my foot down, I'd never outrun them and in any case to do so would only look suspicious, as if I had something to be afraid of. I pulled over and wound my window down as the officer approached.

'Would you step out of the car please, Miss.'

I smiled my most innocent smile. 'Have I done something wrong, officer?'

'Just turn off the engine and step out of the car please.'

'Very well,' I did as I was asked. Both men stood head and shoulders above me, the second officer staying a little back talking into his phone. After a couple of minutes the call ended, the two officers conferred a short distance away from me so I couldn't hear what was being said. The darker skinned of the two approached me, 'We need you to accompany us to the police station; my colleague will drive your car back.' As he spoke he took hold of my arm and began guiding me toward the police car.

'What? There must be some mistake.' I tried to pull my arm free but he just increased his grip.

'Miss Theakston, I am arresting you in connection with the death of Melissa Hartnell. You do not have to say anything but it may harm your defence if you do not mention when questioned something which you later rely on in court. Anything you do say may be given in evidence. Do you understand?'

'What? You can't be serious; that's nothing to do with me.' By now we were up against the police car. I placed my free hand on the side just above the door window and braced myself against the officer's attempt to force me into the back seat.

'Please, Miss Theakston, it'll be much easier if you co-operate.'

'This is all Inspector Munroe's doing, isn't it? He's been determined to convict me of something. This is definitely police harassment.'

'Just get in the car please.' The officer, not willing to use obvious force against a diminutive woman was becoming exasperated.

'I'm not going anywhere without Liliad.'

'Who?'

'She's in the front seat of my car; I insist you fetch her to me – and my handbag or I shall sink shrieking to the ground and accuse you of assaulting me.'

Obviously alarmed at the prospect he called across to his colleague who was just settling himself into my driver's seat. 'Tony, is there someone called Liliad in the front passenger seat?'

Tony looked bemused and grinned. 'There's a large doll.'

I glared at the officer. 'It's a marionette and very valuable. I won't allow you to just leave her in my car. I want her and my handbag, NOW!'

Reluctantly Tony got back out of the car and brought Liliad and my handbag across. Gathering them into my arms I allowed myself to be guided into the back seat of the police car.

Visibly relieved, the officers got into the drivers seats of both cars and pulled away.

◆

Forty five minutes later I was ushered once more into Endover Police Station, the accompanying officer taking hold of my arm to guide me along the corridor. I shook him free. 'I think I know my way by now, officer.' I quickened my pace deliberately to be a few steps in front of him to emphasise the point and allow me to at least feel more in control of the situation, even if it was an illusion.

There was a choice of two interview rooms, one just to my left and the other at the far end of the corridor; that was the one I'd been in when questioned by Inspector Munroe. I hesitated for a second, looking enquiringly at the officer.

'The room at the end of the corridor please, Miss Theakston.'

I raised my eyebrows in mock surprise. 'So, I'm to be graced with DCI Munroe's presence today, am I; the organ grinder instead of the monkey. I am honoured.'

Opening the door the officer pointed to the seat on the far side of the table. 'Please take a seat, a WPC will be with you shortly.' He turned, closing the door behind him.

I didn't sit; I placed my bag on the floor by the chair and stood still clutching Liliad close to me. The room smelt slightly fusty; a rankness to the air from the nervous sweat of the interrogated. A reinforced glass window, the shape of an oversized letterbox, was positioned close to the ceiling and was the only source of natural light. The walls were painted a grey green colour or maybe it was just grime as though the very fabric of the room had absorbed the ill-will and hostility of those held here. I looked down into Liliad's eyes; they were wide open, more than I had ever noticed before, the black pupils seeming to pulse and flash with apprehension.

The door opened and the promised WPC entered, the most stony-faced bulk of a woman I'd ever come across. It was quite clear that she would be no silent ally. I couldn't imagine she'd acquiesce to a polite request for a cup of coffee so didn't bother to ask. Instead I continued my examination of the room.

The floor was badly scuffed especially underneath the chairs from people scraping them back and forth on the hard floor. The table, metal and grey green in keeping with the walls, was ringed by stains from innumerable mugs of coffee and tea. I wondered how DCI Munroe could stand being in here; presumably he spent more hours than any of his victims but then I figured he probably felt at home. His painfully thin frame, long limbs, scrawny neck and dry, scaly skin put me in mind of a reptile. Yes, I could imagine that this confined, murky environment would suit him well. The image was so vivid it wouldn't have surprised me if he'd entered the room on all fours.

I could hear Munroe approaching; the squeak of his shoes on the linoleum of the corridor increasing in volume as he approached. Flinging open the door he didn't even glance at me but kept his eyes firmly on his destination, the chair before him. Slapping a folder onto the table he dragged out his chair, the screech against the floor making me wince and dropped onto it, making a sucking noise as he drew his lips back over his teeth in concentration. I remained standing, Liliad in my arms, her head buried into my shoulder. 'Squeaky shoes, Inspector; my mother always said that was a sign they hadn't been paid for. I do trust you haven't been shoplifting.'

Munroe stared at me, making no attempt to disguise his distaste. 'Just sit down Miss Theakston.'

I did as directed, settling Liliad on my lap facing him. I felt her slight resistance but bent down close to her ear. 'You have to face him too,' my whisper was barely audible even to me.

Looking directly at Munroe I smiled, 'Inspector, Annalee will do nicely; we've known one another for a long time now, I think we can dispense with the formalities.'

'I would rather not, Miss Theakston.'

'Very well, Inspector as you wish but before we go any further, your officer said I was under arrest; if that is the case I insist on having a solicitor present before I will answer any of your questions.'

'I didn't expect anything else, Miss Theakston. Do you have a solicitor or would you like me to arrange for the Duty Solicitor to attend?'

'The Duty Solicitor will be perfectly adequate, I'm sure.'

'Very well,' Munroe nodded to the WPC who left the room, obviously aware of what was required. 'He'll be here shortly.'

We spent the next fifteen minutes in silence, Munroe occasionally flicking through his papers but most of the time leaning back in his chair, staring fixedly at me, occasionally lowering his eyes to look at Liliad who returned his gaze with unblinking intensity. Eventually Munroe asked, 'Would you put the doll down please?'

'No, Inspector I won't.'

Before he could argue, the Duty Solicitor and WPC entered. A squat man in his mid-fifties, his once smart suit did nothing to dispel the overall impression of general neglect as though he was harassed beyond caring. The whiskers on his face didn't look like designer stubble either, rather that he hadn't found time to shave. He held out a hand to me. 'Miss Theakston, I'm Joshua Mellor, the Duty Solicitor. If you so wish, I can represent and advise you during the course of the current investigation but you are at liberty to revert to your own solicitor should you have one and wish to do so.'

I smiled a welcome. 'Thank you, Mr Mellor, I'm sure we'll get along just fine.'

Mr Mellor took his seat beside me and took out his notebook and pen but before settling himself down to business he commented, 'What a beautiful puppet; it's a marionette, isn't it?'

I beamed at him, 'Yes, it is; how refreshing to meet someone who appreciates the craftsmanship that has gone into making her.'

Munroe gave a loud cough. 'If we can dispense with the pleasantries, Mr Mellor, I'd like to get on.'

'Of course, Inspector I apologise.'

Munroe turned on the tape then focussed his attention on me. 'Miss Theakston, you were aware, were you not, that as a person of interest you were not to leave the area without first notifying the police yet it appears that that was exactly what you were endeavouring to do.'

I gave a conciliatory smile, 'I'm so sorry, I misunderstood, I intended to let you have my new address once I was settled; I thought that was sufficient.'

Munroe didn't bother to confirm or deny but carried on. 'You led us and your associates to believe you would be moving somewhere up north yet you were apprehended travelling south. Care to explain?'

'I changed my mind; it's a woman's prerogative.'

Munroe, stony-faced let it drop. 'Tell me, Miss Theakston, have you ever had any contact with Melissa Hartnell?'

I gave an exasperated sigh. 'Oh, Inspector we've been through all this before. No, I have never had any contact with Melissa Hartnell.'

'Then why were you delivering a bouquet of flowers to her apartment a few weeks ago?'

'I wasn't.'

'That's not what the resident of the basement flat tells us. He recognised you from your photograph.'

'What photograph?'

Munroe drew his lips into a congratulatory smirk. 'The one we used to try to identify you after your car accident. You do recall the time you were ostensibly trying to protect my daughter, DS Wilson and myself from the dogs at Barry Mason's cottage? We published the photograph in the national press; it was how we located your parents. Yes, Mark Roberts was quite certain.'

I shifted Liliad on my lap, causing her to lean forward, one arm flopping onto the metal table top with a clunk, for a brief second diverting Munroe's attention giving me time to disguise my surprise. 'Whatever this Mark Roberts thinks, he's mistaken. Why would I be taking flowers to someone I don't know?'

Munroe leant back on his seat, 'I've no idea but I've also had confirmation from an employee at the café on the corner of Cadogan Square that, on the very day the flowers were delivered, you were having coffee in the said café. Something of a coincidence don't you think?'

I opened my mouth to respond but Munroe put up a finger to silence me. 'Don't bother, I know what you're going to say, that it must be someone who looks a lot like you – your doppelganger certainly does get about, doesn't she?'

I scowled, my grip involuntarily tightening around Liliad's waist.

'Were you responsible for the chocolates as well?'

I said nothing.

'You see, we've spoken with Dr Metcalfe, as you might expect. He tells us that Melissa received the flowers and, on Valentines Day, a box of chocolates from an anonymous admirer. She and he were completely baffled by it.'

I simply shrugged.

'Still, let's leave that for now and move on. As you know, we've been trying to trace a Joanne Simons who volunteered to help with the stage make-up at the Manor Road Amateur Theatre. As I believe I've mentioned before, your downstairs neighbour states the woman she bumped into leaving your flat one afternoon bore a striking resemblance to the computer generated image that we put together from descriptions given by members of the theatre group. An odd coincidence, don't you think?'

I remained silent, keeping my face expressionless. Munroe continued, 'I expect your elusive friend must have a doppelganger too.'

I felt Liliad shuffle on my lap, her head dipping slightly downwards as though she was unwilling to look into Munroe's eyes. I decided to take the initiative. 'Inspector, although so far you have not said as much I was told by one of your officers that I was being arrested in connection with the death of Melissa Hartnell. For the benefit of Mr Mellor let's itemise a few things.

One, you have questioned me in this regard before compiling a list of extremely weak circumstantial evidence; for example, you questioned my conversations with the nurse who attended me at St Joseph's, which was merely gossip based on idle curiosity.

Two, you practically accused me of stalking Melissa Hartnell simply because I'd driven past her school on one occasion on my way to the supermarket.

Three, you have questioned my neighbour, managing to put a kind of sinister inference on my collecting some 'dress-up' clothes for the child of a friend of mine. You have also suggested that simply because I enjoyed playing 'dress-up' as a child I must be predisposed in adulthood to assuming various disguises with the intention of conning people.'

I turned to look at Mr Mellor, raising my eyebrows, 'Incredible, don't you agree, Mr Mellor?'

Mr Mellor nodded. 'I must say, Inspector so far it does seem as though you have nothing but circumstantial evidence and even that is suspect. I really don't see that you have much to hold my client on.'

Making no comment Munroe turned his attention from Mr Mellor back to me, as though Mr Mellor hadn't spoken. 'You enjoy cooking do you not, Miss Theakston?'

'*What?*'

Mr Mellor made to speak but Munroe held up his hand. 'Bear with me for a moment. Please answer the question, Miss Theakston.'

'Yes, Inspector I enjoy cooking. Why? Would you like me to invite you to dinner?'

Munroe ignored the jibe and addressed Mr Mellor, adopting a tone of patient explanation. 'As I've said, we've spoken with Mark Roberts, the gentleman in the basement flat at Cadogan Square; he's been most helpful. You may be aware, Mr Mellor that we now have a computer programme that allows us to take the photograph we have of Miss Theakston and get Mark plus members of the amateur theatre group to respond to a group of complete faces (not just facial features any more) to put together a composite of Joanne Simons. These composites form an increasingly accurate image of what a witness saw. It's quite a new technique and results are amazing. It clearly shows that Joanne Simons and Annalee Theakston could easily be one and the same person.'

Raising my voice I insisted, '*But we're not*, are we Inspector? You have no concrete evidence.' I could feel Liliad pressing herself back into my stomach as though trying to increase the distance between herself and Munroe.

'Well, let's just agree to differ on that for the moment. Mark Roberts …'

I sneered, '*Him again!* He has been a busy little bee, hasn't he?'

'Mark Roberts tells us that he bumped into the illusive Joanne Simons. She was visiting Melissa Hartnell, taking a casserole for the dinner they were to have together. I believe you are an accomplished casserole cook, Miss Theakston.'

I said nothing but realised that little nugget had come from Mrs Munroe.

'Like to put in some special ingredients; sun-dried tomatoes, woodland mushrooms?'

Mr Mellor stopped scribbling in his notebook. 'Inspector, where is this line of questioning leading?'

'To the crux of the matter, Mr Mellor; the post mortem and forensic examination revealed that Miss Hartnell had consumed a quantity of psilocybin mushrooms; magic mushrooms to you and I.'

I couldn't prevent a snort of derision. 'Oh please, even if she had, magic mushrooms don't hurt you.'

'You know about these things, do you Miss Theakston? Well, I agree, normally they don't, not that I'm condoning their use but in moderate quantities they are well-tolerated among healthy individuals. Unfortunately in Melissa Hartnell's case things were not so straightforward. Dr Metcalfe informs me that his fiancée had a family history of mental health issues. Our pathologist advises me that psilocybin may well contribute to latent mental health issues making an appearance. In such cases a 'bad trip' is much more likely, for example unpleasant hallucinations, uncontrollable paranoia, reckless behaviour and a transitory state between wakefulness and sleep including trouble with co-ordinating movement.'

Mr Mellor interrupted. 'How long has this information been to hand?'

'Only recently; psilocybin mushrooms and their metabolites are not included in most standard drug screens. It was a lack of any other credible reason for Ms Hartnell's fall that caused us to carry out an extended drug screening.'

Cutting across Munroe I said, 'I'm sorry to break up this fascinating lesson but when did our helpful Mark Roberts say he bumped into Joanne Simons and her casserole?'

Munroe looked at his notes. 'Thursday, 16th June.'

'Then, even if I were Joanne Simons, which I am not, how could that casserole be of relevance. Melissa didn't fall until three weeks later.'

Munroe took a deep breath and spoke as though explaining to a child. 'I wasn't implying it was relevant in that respect.'

'Oh, I see, so you suspect Melissa and Joanne had another meal, another casserole three weeks later. Did Mark Roberts see Joanne arrive on that occasion too?'

'No he did not but that's not to say it didn't happen.'

Mr Mellor interrupted. 'I really do think, Inspector that unless you have something more concrete to report, this interview is at an end.'

Munroe glared at Mellor. 'Then let's go over what I do have. We have two witnesses who, despite denials, have positively identified your client as the woman who delivered flowers to Ms Hartnell's address and was in the local café on the same day. We also have a witness who says he caught her hiding in the car park of Dr Metcalfe's apartment block on the day Melissa Hartnell visited her fiancé and that she visited Nurse Fletcher and made enquiries about Ms Hartnell later that same day. Shortly after that conversation, when she elicited from Nurse Fletcher Ms Hartnell's place of work, she is seen *parked* outside the school, *not just driving past* to the supermarket as she maintains.

Now, let's turn to the mysterious Joanne Simons ignoring for the moment our suspicion that she and Miss Theakston are one and the same. The address given on the application form to the amateur theatre is fictitious.

The membership secretary tells us that Joanne seemed quite distracted during her interview and tour of the theatre, appearing to be on the lookout for someone but that all stopped when Melissa arrived and Joanne positively jumped at the chance of being her assistant.

We then understand from the waitress at the Cadogan Square café that a woman answering Joanne's description met up with Ms Hartnell in the café one Saturday morning and a few days later she is identified by Mark Roberts as the woman meeting Melissa at her apartment for a meal, part of which she appears to be supplying.'

Mr Mellor cut in again. 'That's all very well, Inspector but I really don't think it's enough for a credible case; you still have no actual proof.'

Munroe's irritation was palpable. 'We are still pursuing other enquiries which we feel sure will prove beyond any doubt that Joanne Simons and Annalee Theakston are one and the same but in the meantime Miss Theakston is still very much a person of interest. As such she will remain in custody awaiting further questioning.' He leant towards the tape machine, 'Interview suspended 16th July at 4.15pm.' Turning toward me he said, 'You may have a few moments with your solicitor, Miss Theakston while I arrange a cell for you for the night.' With that he left the room.

Mr Mellor turned to me. 'Is there anything you're not telling me. If I'm to represent you effectively I do need all the facts.'

'No, nothing, Mr Mellor except that Inspector Munroe has never accepted that I wasn't responsible for his daughter being shot in a police raid last year and has even had me questioned about her recent death.'

'Her fall when hiking on Ben Carrick?'

'Exactly; I've never even been to Scotland.' My voice trembled with suppressed emotion, 'and now he's trying to find me guilty of killing someone I've never even met.'

Mr Mellor studied me thoughtfully. 'That's quite an accusation against a respected DCI, Miss Theakston. Let's see how things pan out tomorrow before we start raising issues of police harassment and conflict of interest. Goodbye, I suggest you spend the evening thinking things through; Inspector Munroe obviously feels he has more weighty evidence than that already presented.'

I was left in the room with the surly WPC propped against the wall, staring fixedly ahead. I stood and stretched my legs, clasping Liliad tightly. 'It'll be alright,' I murmured, more for my own reassurance than hers.

CHAPTER 27

I spent an extremely uncomfortable night in the police cell made more uncomfortable by the sullen looks I kept getting from Liliad who made it quite plain that she was not impressed.

'I don't know why you're being so unpleasant; if I hadn't absolutely insisted on your staying with me you'd most likely be sitting on a shelf in some evidence store.'

Liliad simply scowled and turned her head away.

I'd been given a meal, if you could call it that and a mug of tea, then left to myself; the sliding viewing hatch in the door being opened a couple of times during the night so the police could reassure themselves I hadn't committed suicide.

I didn't sleep, too much revolving around my mind. I kept reliving all of it but the bottom line was that I knew I was innocent. It didn't matter that I'd planned to kill

Melissa, the point was I hadn't so they couldn't prove otherwise, could they. I must have dropped off in the early hours from sheer exhaustion because I was awoken by the clank of the cell door being opened and a uniformed sergeant bringing me breakfast.

'When will I be seeing Inspector Munroe again?'

'No idea, Miss but it'll be today, you can be sure of that.'

I sank back down onto the hard mattress and looked at Liliad. 'We should have woken up in Brighton; I could *kill bloody Munroe!*'

It was about ten thirty when I was walked once more to the interview room. Munroe and Mr Mellor were already there, also the WPC propping up the wall again. I almost felt sorry for her.

Mr Mellor spoke first. 'Sorry for the slight delay, Miss Theakston; I was held up in the office.'

I gave him a half smile accepting his apology. No point getting his back up. On the other hand, getting Munroe's back up was positively pleasurable.

'Couldn't you have left that doll in the cell, Miss Theakston; it's very distracting.'

'As I've said before, she's very valuable. I've no intention of leaving her where she could be stolen.'

Munroe glared, 'This is a police station!'

'I know; I rest my case.'

Refusing to rise to the bait Munroe switched on the tape and gave the usual introduction. Pulling his chair closer to the table he said, 'Let's start with Joanne Simons.'

'Oh, for God's sake; how many more times; I am *not* Joanne Simons. Do you have any evidence proving otherwise, fingerprints for example?'

'My, we are a little touchy this morning; didn't you sleep well?'

Mr Mellor broke in. 'Inspector, cut the sarcasm please.'

'Very well, I apologise, Miss Theakston but as you mention fingerprints let's start there. It's a very strange thing that despite working backstage Joanne appears to have left no fingerprints. We've eliminated all the cast and backstage helpers …'

'That must have taken some time.'

'Yes, it did but in the interests of getting to the truth we can be very thorough. As I was saying there were no prints unaccounted for; it was as though she'd never been there. However, when we spoke to the cast of the show they told us that Joanne always wore fine, white linen gloves. She said she had very sensitive skin and could get an allergic reaction to the substances used.'

I sat back, adjusting Liliad on my lap. 'How unfortunate.'

'Indeed but we do have another line of enquiry so all is not lost. Joanne filled out an application form for the theatre, the one bearing the fictitious address. It was handwritten and has been kept with the secretary's papers; who assures us that it would only have passed through her hands and that of the applicant, ergo Joanne Simons.'

At that precise moment there was a polite knock on the door and a technician entered. 'My colleague here will take your fingerprints, Miss Theakston. Please co-operate.'

I looked enquiringly at Mr Mellor who nodded. Munroe noticing the exchange continued, 'We have every right to take your fingerprints and a DNA sample should I so require; we do not need your permission.'

It only took a few moments to complete the procedure. Once the technician had left the room Munroe began again. 'Your fingerprints will now be compared with those on the application form but just in case that is inconclusive we are also having our handwriting expert examine the form and make a comparison with examples of your handwriting that we recently obtained from your place of work. I wonder what that will elicit.'

I could feel a prickle of nervous tension run down my back as I stared at Munroe. I needed time to think. I wiped a hand across my brow, 'It's very airless in here; may I have a cup of water please?'

Munroe signalled to the WPC who immediately left the room. He was about to continue when Mr Mellor butted in. 'I think Miss Theakston could do with a break, Inspector. May I have a few moments with my client, alone?'

Munroe grudgingly agreed. 'I will return shortly, Miss Theakston.' He pushed back his chair, switched off the tape then turned and left the room.

Mr Mellor turned on his chair toward me, his face deadly serious. 'Miss Theakston, if your fingerprints match those on the application form filled in by Joanne Simons and if the police handwriting expert concludes that the handwriting is yours it's going to be very difficult to continue to maintain that you are *not* Joanne Simons. However, that alone does not prove that you killed Ms Hartnell on the day in question. Do you have an alibi for that day?'

I shook my head.

'Pity, it would make things much easier. I suggest you come up with a credible reason why you adopted the persona of Joanne Simons and we'll leave the police to prove that you/she was there on the night of the murder.'

Just at that moment the WPC re-entered the room bearing my requested glass of water. Mr Mellor stood, 'I'll leave you alone to think things through.' Gathering up his briefcase and the notes he'd been making he departed leaving me alone with the sour-faced WPC.

I turned Liliad around on my lap so that she was facing me and lowered my head so that our foreheads were touching. Closing my eyes I forced myself to regulate my breathing until I felt a calm descend. Raising my head I looked deep into Liliad's eyes assessing my reflection in her pupils and I knew what I would say.

I took a couple of long swallows of the water; it was slightly tepid; the bitch obviously hadn't bothered to get it chilled from the machine but brought simply tap water. No matter, I didn't intend to be here much longer. Munroe could *not* put me at the scene of the crime because I hadn't been there; I had *not* murdered Melissa so there could be no evidence that I had. The thought reassured me although when I whispered my conclusion to Liliad her head dropped onto her chest and she refused to meet my gaze.

Twenty minutes later Munroe and Mr Mellor returned, Munroe holding a couple of sheets of A4 paper which he tucked into the folder as he sat. I looked enquiringly at Mr Mellor but he studiously didn't return my look. Munroe turned on the tape recorder. 'Miss Theakston, I trust your little chat with your solicitor has helped to clarify your position but in case you still have any doubts as to what would be in your best interests I must inform you that we have a positive fingerprint match and our handwriting expert has concluded that the handwriting on the theatre application form and the sample we took from your place of work are one and the same.'

Simply because I knew he found it extremely aggravating I turned Liliad around on my lap so that she was facing him. I also shuffled her forward, placing both her arms on the table top and tilting her head slightly so that her eyes widened, her stare unblinking. I then put on my most contrite expression, my voice humble and apologetic. 'Inspector, I've been very silly but perhaps I might explain …'

'Please do, Miss Theakston; I'm all ears.'

Lowering my head as if in embarrassment, my voice barely above a whisper, 'As you know, I was aware of Melissa and that she was Dr Metcalfe's fiancée from my time in St Joseph's. Dr Metcalfe has her photograph on his desk.'

Munroe interrupted. 'Speak up please, for the tape.'

Only raising my voice slightly I continued. 'She was *so* pretty and Nurse Fletcher sang her praises too, about how lovely her personality was. I was envious but not in a bad way, I simply wanted to be like her, I thought I could learn from her. I've so few friends, well, since I lost Lily ...' I could sense Munroe stiffen, barely suppressing the urge to strike me. '... I really don't have any friends; it's very lonely.' I paused, bending down to my handbag, the few seconds effectively hidden under the table allowing me to compose my features and keep my thoughts in order. I came up clutching a tissue, sniffling into it.

'Anyway, I wanted to get close to her, get to know her in the hope that we could become friends but I was scared too; I didn't want Dr Metcalfe to know, I was sure he'd prevent it and in any case, if Melissa knew I'd been treated in St Joseph's and by Dr Metcalfe she probably wouldn't want to know me anyway so that's why I became Joanne Simons.'

Mr Mellor was looking at me intently, occasionally making notes as I spoke but Inspector Munroe merely leant back in his chair and gave a slow handclap. Mr Mellor snapped at him. 'Inspector, that response is most inappropriate when my client is doing her best to explain her motives. Do I have to ask you again to cut the sarcasm?'

'I apologise Mr Mellor and to you, Miss Theakston. Tell me, why have you persistently denied that you were Joanne Simons if your intentions were as innocent as you claim?'

I shot him a look of pure malevolence. '*Why do you think, Inspector?* When I learnt that she'd died I knew from bitter experience that if you knew I'd had any association with her you'd immediately suspect me of involvement.' By now I'd raised my voice to just below the level of a shout. 'After all, you hounded me when Lily was shot in *your* police raid; despite being unable to prove anything you made every effort to keep us apart so that when Lily went up to Scotland she just about stopped all contact with me and then, when Lily had her "accident"…; I emphasised the word to make the point that foul play was still not proven. '… I had Mrs Munroe calling round to my flat on several occasions asking what can only be described as searching questions. Were you aware she had called on me? Was she acting on your instructions?'

Mr Mellor pulled himself into a more upright position. 'Is this true, Inspector? Has your wife been 'interrogating' my client?'

Munroe, visibly disconcerted leant forward placing his arms on the table in imitation of Liliad, his hands clenched into fists so tightly that the white of his knuckles was clearly visible. 'No, I was not aware of my wife's involvement.'

By now I really was shouting. 'So how did you know what ingredients I like to put in my casseroles? It seems that you can be economical with the truth too, Inspector.' I leant forward which caused Liliad to sort of slide along the table top until her face was inches from Munroe's. 'But let's not worry about that now.' I turned to Mr Mellor. 'Because to top it all I'm hauled in here by the Inspector's sidekick, DS Wilson and practically accused of murdering Lily on

Ben Carrick despite his being unable to produce a shred of proof; once again the police suspicions are based on the flimsiest of circumstantial evidence and you wonder why I didn't dare disclose my little subterfuge where Melissa is concerned! What the hell else does anyone expect?'

I grabbed hold of Liliad as I stood pushing my chair back with such force it clattered to the floor, startling everyone. I turned away from them all and lay my forehead against the wall, my body wracked with sobs.

Mr Mellor stood, presumably to assume more authority, 'In view of my client's distressed state I think we should at least take a break, Inspector or rather, either charge my client or let her go but I must say I don't consider that you have so far proved that she has any case to answer.'

Munroe also stood, stretching the kinks out of his back so that he stood at his full height of six feet four, dwarfing the squat Mr Mellor. 'I agree to a break, for all our sakes, but I wish to continue my questioning. Further evidence has recently come to light...' I turned from the wall as a tingle of shock and disbelief ran through my body. Munroe's look met mine. '...an eye witness no less. I feel that needs pursuing.'

He turned off the tape, 'I suggest we all get some lunch and resume at two thirty. The WPC will see you back to the cell, Miss Theakston.' With that he left the room.

I turned to Mr Mellor in confusion and query but he merely shrugged. 'We'll have to wait and see, Miss Theakston,' he said, reading my mind.

CHAPTER 28

The WPC walked me back to the cell, 'A meal will be brought down to you shortly.' She turned without another word or any change of expression and left. I slumped onto the unyielding mattress that passed for a bed, carefully placing Liliad beside me. 'What does he mean; eye witness?'

Liliad sat mute, letting her head drop onto her chest and her eyes close. I sat observing her for a while, noting once more the incredibly soft texture of her eyelashes as they lay against her highly defined cheek bones. She was so beautiful; the one truly precious thing that I possessed; I couldn't bear to lose her.

Eventually my meal arrived on its plastic tray with its plastic plate and plastic cutlery – no consideration for single use plastics fouling the environment it seemed. The food might just as well have been plastic for all the taste it

imparted but I forced about half of it down; it was important I didn't weaken in body or mind. Once finished I had
nothing I could do but wait; it was pointless to sit trying
to work out who this eye witness could be although I had
my suspicions but I knew whatever they claimed it would
be a lie – *I simply wasn't there.*

Just before two thirty I was once more propelled down
that miserable corridor; Munroe obviously didn't want to
waste time. I was the first to enter the interview room
followed immediately by my 'personal' WPC who took up
sentry duty in her usual spot; to the left of the door facing
forward. I was so sick of her surly indifference I walked
over to her as she stared fixedly ahead. Standing directly in
front, my face only inches from her own I raised my hand
and carefully picked at the breast pocket of her uniform.
'Whoops, seems you've dropped some cottage pie down
your front.' She glanced down involuntarily. ' We can't
have you looking scruffy in front of Inspector Munroe,
can we?' I smirked and turned back toward my seat just
as DCI Munroe and Mr Mellor entered.

'Take a seat, Miss Theakston.' Munroe was straight to
business, turning on the tape and giving details of date,
time and who was in the room. He launched straight in.
'Miss Theakston, where were you on the evening of the
seventh of July?'

I made to place Liliad on my lap facing Munroe as
before but felt her resistance so instead held her against
my chest, her back to Munroe and her head resting on

my shoulder as though she were asleep. Absent-mindedly I patted her back as she lay there, the comforting rhythm that a mother gives her child; not that I'd ever experienced any such thing from *my* mother.

'I'm waiting.' Munroe tapped his pen against the closed folder that lay once more on the table between us.

I sighed. 'It's so long ago, Inspector; I really can't remember,' Noting his frustration I added, 'but I expect I was at home, I am most nights.'

'Can anyone verify that?'

'I shouldn't think so, it was most likely just myself and Liliad but I don't suppose her word will be good enough.'

Munroe scowled, 'Well, that's unfortunate because we have a witness who puts you inside Melissa Hartnell's apartment on that night, or rather I should say, puts your alter ego, Joanne Simons in her apartment.'

'I suppose this is the, oh so helpful, Mark Roberts.'

'No, Miss Theakston it isn't. Care to hazard a guess?'

Mr Mellor interrupted. '*Inspector*, quit the games.'

'I'm sorry, Mr Mellor I was under the impression that your client liked playing games. Never mind ...' He looked directly at me, locking his eyes with mine ensuring my complete attention. '... it was Dr Metcalfe; a very credible witness I think you'll agree.'

My jaw dropped in astonishment as I sat for quite a few seconds like a gaping fish before I shut my mouth. I'd felt Liliad flinch at Dr Metcalfe's name as she pressed more firmly against me. Sheer reflex caused me to pat her back again in reassurance although I felt none myself. The silence in the room grew until Mr Mellor said, 'Care to give us some more detail, Inspector?'

Munroe wriggled slightly on his chair as though trying to get some comfort from its unforgiving seat and opened the folder, extracting a typed two page document. 'I have here Dr Metcalfe's statement, it makes for interesting reading. You see, when we arrived at Ms Hartnell's apartment on the night of her death we found the table set for two. A casserole adorned the centre but only partly consumed as was the bottle of wine and only one plate and one glass had been used. It looked as though whoever had been intending to dine with Ms Hartnell had left rather abruptly before eating anything but knowing, as we do, what was in the casserole that's hardly surprising, is it?' Munroe looked directly at me but I kept all expression from my features.

'In his statement, Dr Metcalfe explains that he was calling on his fiancée unexpectedly as he'd just heard that his latest academic paper had been received to great acclaim by the medical profession and he wanted to share the good news with her but when he got there he could see someone else standing at her front balcony window, looking out over the gardens and fountain. He recognised her as Joanne Simons.'

Mr Mellor looked enquiringly at Munroe who explained, 'He'd met Joanne one evening at the Manor Road Theatre when he'd gone to collect Melissa, so was certain it was her.'

Mr Mellor looked toward me for an explanation. '*It wasn't me*; I admit I was in the guise of Joanne Simons on the evening Mark Roberts bumped into me but I've never been back since.'

'And we're supposed to believe that, are we especially in view of all the other lies you've told during the course of this interview?' Munroe almost smirked but forced his lips under control and instead produced a thin smile. 'One other thing, which I'm sure you'll claim is merely circumstantial, Mr Mellor but circumstantial evidence does, in my humble experience, have a habit of stacking up. When we searched Miss Theakston's flat our officer found several books relating to food and food plants in her kitchen.'

I cut across, my derision evident in my tone, 'I expect he would; it's a food preparation area for God's sake.'

'Indeed, but they weren't all recipe books. One was to do with foraging, another exclusively about various funghi and it appeared you'd even borrowed a couple from the local library on similar topics. You're going to have quite a fine if you've forgotten to return them – I mean, your being in such haste to leave the area.'

I said nothing.

'You see, with the help of our pathologist and the background Dr Metcalfe was able to give us as to the mental history of Ms Hartnell's family what we think happened is this. Ms Hartnell had a guest for dinner who provided the main course, a casserole stuffed full of mushrooms, many of which were the infamous magic sort, of which it appears poor Ms Hartnell consumed a large quantity, probably in disappointment at her mystery guest leaving the party so soon.

The effect of the mushrooms takes approximately one and a half hours to appear, plenty of time for someone to get well away from the scene. Dr Metcalfe tells us that Ms Hartnell suffered from anxiety and occasional bouts of depression; she was of a generally nervous disposition and had what he termed a 'fragile mental state' and after all, he should know. Her not being aware of what she was consuming, meant that she was unable to prepare herself for their effects; hallucinations, paranoia, lack of co-ordination of movement etcetera.

We can, of course, only surmise but it seems likely that Ms Hartnell had what is colloquially termed a 'bad trip'. We will never know what she faced in the hours that followed; what hallucinatory terrors awaited her but it seems likely that she climbed up onto her balcony wall, losing her balance as she tried to walk along it and fell which resulted in her being impaled on the railings below. A terrible way to meet one's Maker, I'm sure you'll agree.'

Silence followed Munroe's monologue, all of us contemplating the obscene image his description evoked. Munroe stood towering over me. 'Miss Theakston, I am formerly charging you with the murder of Ms Melissa Hartnell.'

I turned in panic to Mr Mellor, '*But I didn't do it!*'

'Save that for the trial, Miss Theakston.' Munroe gathered up his papers and left the room.

CHAPTER 29

I sit by the window gazing out at the manicured garden, Liliad balanced on the window cill next to me. This is the same room that I occupied when Mrs Munroe visited bringing Liliad back, carried in a plastic shopping bag. I wonder what Liliad is thinking as she too gazes out of the window but she doesn't speak much these days, preferring to keep her thoughts to herself.

My Counsel did an adequate job at the trial advocating that if it was my intention to murder Melissa then I'd used a pretty uncertain method for an otherwise intelligent person; there could be no guarantee that her 'bad trip' would lead to her death. At best it could only be argued that I'd meant to cause her harm, give her a real fright but the main aid to the charge being reduced from murder to manslaughter had been Dr Metcalfe. I don't think DCI Munroe was very pleased when Dr Metcalfe appeared for the Defence rather than the Prosecution especially as he seemed determined to refute the psychiatric assessment provided by the Prosecution's expert witness.

Dr Metcalfe was adamant that I was suffering from psychosis and as such was unable to exercise self-control, rational judgement or indeed, to understand the nature of my actions.

As I'd purportedly killed his fiancée, if anyone had an axe to grind it was Dr Metcalfe. The jury took this obvious fact on board clearing me of murder but convicting me of manslaughter with the recommendation that I was committed to a mental hospital rather than prison. Fortunately, in handing down sentence the judge concurred and so here I was, back in St Joseph's.

I was not, this time, to be under the care of Dr Metcalfe for obvious reasons; another psychiatrist, a Dr Rowlands was appointed to oversee my treatment but he unfortunately died in a road traffic accident within a couple of months of my internment. Dr Metcalfe being the only other professional within miles with extensive experience in treating psychopaths he therefore took over and as no-one seemed to check on the goings-on at St Joseph's, no-one objected.

Betty Fletcher is once again my main nurse but that's where the similarity ends. She's no longer the comforting grandmother figure she was before; now she treats me with civility and conscientious care but with a coldness that is palpable; she certainly no longer calls me 'Dearie' and spends as little time as possible in my company.

On the other hand, I spend a lot of time in therapy with Dr Metcalfe who's devoting a considerable part of each week to my treatment.

The door opens and Nurse Fletcher enters. 'Time for your session with Dr Metcalfe, Annalee.'

I immediately stand and follow her out of the room; in view of the frosty atmosphere I make a point of complying with all I'm asked; there'd be little to gain from being antagonistic.

Dr Metcalfe's room is just as I'd remembered it; the cosy lighting, coffee machine cheerfully gurgling in the corner, his mahogany leather topped desk and swivel chair. Melissa's photograph is still on his desk.

'Annalee please, take a seat.' He indicates the cosy armchair opposite his own. He doesn't sit behind his desk to hold these sessions, preferring the relaxed, informal approach as though we're sitting in his apartment lounge having a sociable chat. 'Coffee?' It's a perfunctory question; he knows I always say yes. Good coffee is one of my weaknesses.

We sit for a moment, sipping our coffee, quietly appreciating its quality until Dr Metcalfe breaks the companionable silence. 'You know, Annalee it's been six months and you're still maintaining your innocence. Don't you think it's time you acknowledged the truth?'

Slowly I replaced my cup onto its saucer and looked unwaveringly at him. 'Will it aid my release from here?'

Dr Metcalfe shook his head. 'Not in itself, no.'

'Then I admit to nothing because that *is* the truth.'

Moving across the room to get a fresh coffee Dr Metcalfe allowed himself a slight sigh. Keeping his back to me he said, 'I always knew you were Joanne Simons although I didn't tell that to the police.'

Surprised I had to steady my hand to prevent rattling my cup onto its saucer as I replaced it. 'I beg your pardon.'

He turned to face me. 'I knew Joanne Simons was you the moment we met that evening in the theatre.'

'Then why didn't you say anything? Let Melissa know I was a fake.'

'It suited my purpose and anyway, I was intrigued to know what you were up to. I like playing games too. Another coffee?'

My mind was whirring, trying to make sense of what he was saying. 'What? Oh, no, thank you.' What did he mean, it suited his purpose? I chewed at my bottom lip considering his words and the underlying threat they held.

Having poured himself another coffee he returned to his armchair, settling himself deep into its ample cushions he calmly crossed his legs in relaxed manner, taking a sip before he met my eyes. 'Yes, it was quite entertaining watching you manipulate your way into Melissa's life; I must give you full marks for perseverance and attention to detail, even if Melissa *was* an easy target – very gullible, too trusting for her own good.'

I stared at him; he was talking about Melissa as though he had no feelings for her at all. A worrying thought crossed my mind. 'Tell me, Dr Metcalfe what actually happened to Dr Rowlands?'

'A car accident.'

'Yes, I know but what caused it?'

Dr Metcalfe gave what was obviously a well-rehearsed reply. 'The brakes apparently failed. He was terrible about maintaining that old car; I'd expressed my concern to him lots of times.'

'Is that what you told the police?'

'But of course; such a tragedy but as they say, 'every cloud has a silver lining' for someone and here we are again, Annalee.' He smiled benevolently.

'Indeed we are, Dr Metcalfe.' I returned his smile, pretending to acknowledge that we were both in this thing together but just to be sure I asked, 'Why did you speak up for me at the trial?'

As though savouring the moment he replied, 'My my, you do have an inflated opinion of yourself, don't you. I wasn't speaking up for you; I simply didn't want you shut away in some prison for years, it would have been such a waste. I wanted you here, in St Joseph's so we can continue the game.'

'What game?' I rubbed at my arms, trying to dispel the goose bumps that had risen, catching my fingers on the razor blade scars from my adolescence.

'The game you've been playing since childhood and that you brought to my door here at St Joseph's after your car accident.'

'I don't understand.' My voice, barely above a whisper was another calculated lie for I knew only too well.

'No, I don't suppose you do but you will in time.' He reached across and pressed the intercom button. 'Nurse Fletcher, we've finished today's session. Would you take Annalee back to her room please.'

I sat motionless as we both waited for Nurse Fletcher and all the time Dr Metcalfe sat watching me, saying nothing. I rose immediately the door opened suddenly feeling an overwhelming urge to get out of there and think things through with Liliad.

◆

I strode across my hospital room, throwing myself on my bed face down and buried my head in my pillow, anger boiling inside me. How dare Dr Metcalfe compete with me; this was *my* game. So, I'd understand 'in time' would I? Oh no, Dr Metcalfe, believe me, I understand *now* only too well.

I thumped the pillow in frustration, waiting for the rage to pass. After a while I turned and sat, knowing I needed to calmly discuss the matter with Liliad. Propping the pillows up behind me I wrapped my arms around my drawn up knees, my eyes still focussed downwards. 'I don't like this, Liliad; I don't know how to handle it.' I waited for her reply but was met with silence. 'Please, Liliad don't be like that; I need your help.' I looked across at the window cill.

It was empty!

I leapt off the bed and frantically searched the room. The window wasn't open so she couldn't have fallen out; ridiculously I began opening all the cupboards and drawers and then got down on the floor to search under the bed and chairs. Nothing.

I slumped down where I was. How was I to manage without Liliad to confide in, to bounce ideas off? She was the only one I could truly be myself with.

The door opened and Nurse Fletcher came in bearing my evening pills. 'Nurse, do you know where my marionette is?'

'Dr Metcalfe had her removed.'

'Why?'

'I expect he feels you need to manage without her.' Her reply was so matter of fact, making no allowance for how I might feel. 'Here, take your tablets.' She held out the glass of water and small container of pills. I put my hands behind my back. 'I'm not taking anything until I get her back.'

She shrugged. 'As you wish; does that include your dinner?' With that she made to leave the room, turning at the door. 'You realise you'll only delay your recovery if you don't co-operate with the treatment.'

I scowled at her, as if I had any hope of ever leaving this place. After all, Dr Metcalfe had let me out once believing I was 'cured' but I wasn't, was I; Lily could testify to that. As the door closed behind Nurse Fletcher I walked slowly toward the chair by the window. Settling myself into it I began to plan my way forward.

CHAPTER 30

I didn't take the pills, I didn't have dinner and I didn't go to bed that night; instead I sat in the chair and watched as the evening sun cast its dying rays across the garden, eventually turning the sky crimson as it sank below the horizon. My window was the old-fashioned sash type but barred in case an inmate was tempted to throw themselves out; out from the four storey height to mash their brain and shatter their bones on the flagstones below as a silent indictment of the hospital's efficacy.

It had been a warm, humid day so I'd pushed the lower frame up and the upper frame down a fraction to let in what air I could. As the day drew to a close the temperature had dropped and a gentle breeze sneaked into the room, caressing my bare arms as gently as a stroke from a feather as I sat motionless in my chair.

Another hour passed and a three quarter moon rose over the earth, its shape sharply delineated against the dark black blue of the night sky as though it was a precision cut-out fashioned with a razor blade. Its face was the colour of fresh snow reflecting its coldness back into my heart.

As I sat in the darkness I slowly became attuned to the sounds of the night; the bark of a fox, the grunting snuffle of a hedgehog on the lawn, the whoosh of an owl as it swooped on its prey and the terrified shriek of its victim. I felt I was a part of this dark world; a silent stalker, the only indication of my presence being the glint of my eyes.

An incoherent shout from an inmate brought an abrupt stop to my imaginings, callously reminding me of my current reality and I felt my entire body rebel.

By the time Nurse Fletcher arrived in the morning I was calmly focussed. I swallowed my morning pills and accepted my breakfast.

'I'm glad to see you've come to your senses,' Nurse Fletcher gave me a stern look, 'let's have no more of last night's nonsense.'

I bowed my head in contrition but said nothing.

'Get yourself showered and changed, Dr Metcalfe wants to see you at eleven.'

I nodded and tucked into my cereal.

Telling me to get 'changed' was something of a euphemism as there was no real change available, only more of the same but cleaner; jogging pants, T-shirt and when cold, a sweatshirt; a kind of uniform for the criminally insane. Still, I did as I was told and was ready and waiting by eleven o'clock.

I kept my eyes fixed ahead as Nurse Fletcher and I made the so familiar journey down the long corridors and through the various security doors to the hallowed region of the consultants' rooms. There were four on Dr Metcalfe's floor although one, that which had belonged to Dr Rowlands, was still unoccupied. As we went through the final security door the paintwork changed from the depressing purple brown colour of the inmates living areas, devoid of any adornment, to a cheerful aquamarine, the walls now sporting framed paintings of tranquil scenes. I paused by one depicting a loch framed by mountains reminding me of Scotland. I viewed it with a sense of nostalgia; my trip there really had been an achievement.

Nurse Fletcher ushered me into Dr Metcalfe's room and left immediately. Without waiting to be asked I walked over to the coffee machine and poured myself a cup and then took up position in my usual chair. Dr Metcalfe raised his eyebrows in slight surprise but didn't comment.

Silently he poured himself a coffee and sat opposite surveying me over the rim of his cup. After a few moments he said, 'I'd like to continue where we left off yesterday; if you recall we were talking about your liking for playing games.'

'I'm not sure what you mean; what sort of games? Ludo, chess, snakes and ladders?'

He gave a slight smile. 'I think you know what I mean. Your whole life is a game, isn't it? The dressing up, the manipulation of others, your fictitious pasts; I wonder who the real Annalee Theakston is.'

I said nothing. He paused for a while, then moved across to his desk and picked up the photograph of Melissa. He studied it thoughtfully for a few seconds then turned it towards me. 'Do you feel anything over Melissa's death?'

I held his gaze and considered. 'We don't all have an inborn empathy with others however desirable society might consider that to be. I can manufacture the feelings if I so wish but it's not an involuntary reflex action so no, I feel nothing but then, I didn't kill Melissa.'

He smiled very slightly and replaced the photograph. As he returned to his chair he said quietly, 'No, I know you didn't.'

I wasn't sure I'd heard him correctly, his voice was so low but as I watched him I knew I hadn't misheard. I recalled his attitude towards Melissa when I'd listened in to their conversation at the café in the Mall; I recalled the dark figure I'd seen lurking in the trees by the theatre car park, that flash of red silk lining to his jacket. I remembered how put out Melissa had seemed when he turned up at the theatre unexpectedly and the disquiet she'd expressed but then dismissed over his plans for her future.

I studied Dr Metcalfe as he sat before me and I knew, beyond any doubt. After all, it takes one to know one.

Placing his coffee cup on the table between us, he settled further back in his chair, a self-congratulatory smile on his face. 'Aren't you going to ask me how I know?'

I shrugged as though it was of no importance to me. Looking slightly put out he leant forward for his coffee and took another sip, replacing the empty cup back on the table. 'I knew that using the magic mushrooms was a gamble, there was no way to be sure their effect would result in her death but I figured it didn't matter either way; there's always something else to try. If you have the patience you get there in the end but then, you'd know all about that wouldn't you.'

I tilted my head on one side and looked at him enquiringly.

'Lily – it took more than one go, didn't it?'

I kept my face impassive and said nothing; if he thought I would ever admit to that he *was* insane. Dr Metcalfe continued, obviously enjoying himself. 'The police were bound to suspect you of Melissa's death, especially with your past history with Inspector Munroe. It helped that I was able to advise them that the method was very much that of a woman's. You see, women tend to be more creative and poisoning, well near enough in this case, is very much a woman's choice; no physical strength required and the ability to be well away from the scene before anything happens. As I told the Inspector, women killers also tend to be well-educated and often come from abusive backgrounds such as alcoholic parents. You fitted the profile to a 'T'.'

'So what do you want from me, Dr Metcalfe; a congratulatory pat on the back?'

He grinned, got up from his chair and walked across the room to the large free-standing cupboard against the far wall. He reached into the cupboard, his back effectively blocking my view. Turning round with a flourish he dangled Liliad out before him on the ends of her strings, her feet not quite touching the ground. 'Tell me, Annalee what's the significance of this puppet to you? What role does she play in your games? She's remarkably like you; the hairstyle, the eyes. Did you have her specially made?'

Her eyes wide, her pupils black like the still waters at the bottom of a fetid well, Liliad's head turned upwards to glare at Dr Metcalfe then turned back to me with a venomous look. Our eyes locked and it took all my strength to refrain from jumping out of the chair and wrestling her free of Dr Metcalfe's grasp. Instead, I merely shrugged, 'Oh, I wondered where she'd gone.'

Dr Metcalfe attempted to dance her around the coffee table, making a complete fist of it but talking to me all the time. 'You call her Liliad, don't you, after the two women you murdered?'

Again I said nothing, merely observed him.

'Let me see now; Addie, that was your brother's girlfriend; she drowned as I recall and you were the only person present at that tragic time, only nine years old too, quite remarkable and then, of course, Lily, DCI Munroe's daughter. Now that was an achievement, such patience and no proof whatever to put you at the scene although Inspector Munroe definitely has his suspicions and of course, let's not forget poor Nurse Debbie, bludgeoned unconscious just as she was having a quiet smoke. I saw you from my window walking across the grounds shortly before she passed by. That was quite a leap forward, being physically violent. It's no wonder no-one suspected you, quite out of character. Was it a practice run for Lily?'

I kept my expression blank. 'Dr Metcalfe, if you considered me capable of such acts why did you discharge me after my previous treatment? You must have known the risk you were taking.'

'Oh indeed, I did but that was the whole point. You were providing such excellent material for my latest academic treatise and the more I studied you the more I became curious about what it must actually *feel* like to do the things you do. I had to find out for myself; I'm afraid poor Melissa was simply collateral damage but she'll be pleased to know she played a vital role in my research. It was extremely stimulating to plan and then to carry out the dastardly deed. Killing her wasn't my intention, I expected her to simply have a bad experience but when I discovered what had happened the thrill was almost orgasmic. Is that how it is for you? Is that the ultimate reward of the game?'

As I looked into his eyes I knew, without a shadow of doubt that while he was still here I would never get out of St Joseph's. I glanced down at Liliad who was now slumped on the floor, her strings draped carelessly on her head as Dr Metcalfe had dropped them.

He returned to his chair, leaning back in contentment having played his trump card.

'Another coffee?' I asked.

''Please.'

I rose, picking up his cup from the coffee table. As I passed, with my free hand I scooped up from his desk the heavy glass paperweight that sat on a pile of papers. Walking behind his chair to the coffee machine I noted with fascination the gleaming white of his scalp where he'd parted his dark hair, a perfectly straight line on which I focussed. I raised the paperweight and brought it down with all my strength again and again and again, the rhythm intoxicating and I didn't stop until his skull was nothing more than a conglomeration of splintered bone and brain matter.

Letting the bloodied paperweight drop to the floor I stood for a few moments, surveying my handiwork then walked across to his en suite bathroom where I washed the splattered blood and brain from my hands and face.

Returning to the room with a piece of water soaked cloth, I picked Liliad up and gently wiped from her face and legs the splatters that had reached her. I smiled down into her eyes and was gratified to see her smiling back. Settling into the armchair, Liliad on my lap, we both contemplated the macabre figure of Dr Metcalfe, still propped upright in his chair with the jellied mass of his brain slowly trickling down his face, the only sound in the room the normality of the seductive gurgling of the coffee machine.

'He was right, Liliad, it is almost orgasmic and really rather satisfying. Game to us I think.'

BIOGRAPHY

Having retired Lynne Fox wrote her debut novel as nothing more than a personal challenge; 'I simply wanted to know if I could actually finish something for once.' 'Heads I Win, Tails You Lose' garnered praise and several requests for a sequel and so 'It's All in the Game' was born.

Lynne lives in Welwyn Garden City.

www.ingramcontent.com/pod-product-compliance
Lightning Source LLC
Chambersburg PA
CBHW050842190726

48286CB00007B/2195